BEDDED FOR
THE SPANIARD'S
PLEASURE

BEDDED FOR THE SPANIARD'S PLEASURE

BY

CAROLE MORTIMER

MILLS & BOON™

Pure reading pleasure™

First published in Great Britain 2009
Large Print edition 2009
Harlequin Mills & Boon Limited,
Eton House, 18-24 Paradise Road,
Richmond, Surrey TW9 1SR

© Carole Mortimer 2009

ISBN: 978 0 263 20604 3

Set in Times Roman 16½ on 19¼ pt.
16-0709-48242

Printed and bound in Great Britain
by CPI Antony Rowe, Chippenham, Wiltshire

CHAPTER ONE

'CAN I help— You!' Cairo's pleasant query broke off in a gasp, and she came to a startled halt in the driveway as she easily recognized the man stepping out of the car a short distance away.

No!

This couldn't be!

This man could not be here, of all places!

Cairo had been lazing beside the pool, sunbathing, when she'd seen the silver car slowly moving up the winding, narrow road with access only to this villa in the South of France. She had already been on her feet and pulling on a thigh-length black T-shirt over her bikini when she'd heard the car stop outside. Forcing down her irritation at this intrusion, she had hurried towards the driveway to tell the driver that they had obviously lost their way.

But nothing—nothing!—could have prepared her for the man who now stood beside the car, sunglasses pushed up into the dark silkiness of his hair, as he looked across the car's bonnet at her through narrowed lids.

If she was surprised to see him, then he looked no more pleased to see her, his mouth tightening grimly even as he lifted a hand to move the sunglasses back into place over those eyes of sky-blue.

'Cairo,' he greeted her with a terse nod of his head.

Cairo couldn't speak. Couldn't move. In fact, this whole situation felt completely unreal!

'Cat got your tongue, Cairo?' he taunted in his huskily familiar transatlantic drawl, dark brows quirked above those sunglasses. 'Or maybe it's just been so long that you don't remember me?' he taunted.

Not remember him…?

Of course Cairo remembered him!

It might be eight years since she had so much as set eyes on this man, but what women ever—truthfully!—forgot her very first lover? No, Cairo had never completely forgotten Raphael Antonio Miguel Montero. How could she have, when Rafe Montero was the half-American, half-Spanish A-list actor who had been known all over the world for the last fifteen years, and more recently as director of the Oscar-winning film *Work of Art*?

He regarded her coldly now. 'Do you really have nothing to say to me, Cairo?'

'I said all that I needed to say to you the last time we met!' she snapped, even as she desperately tried to make sense of the fact that Rafe was here at all, at this remote villa situated in the hills above the picturesque town of Grasse.

Rafe grimaced as he moved to the back of the car. 'It's been so long I've forgotten,' he drawled before lifting up the boot of the car to begin taking bags from inside and placing them beside him on the driveway.

Cairo could only stand and stare at the man

who had once filled her twenty-year-old heart, as well as her bed.

Now aged in his late thirties, if anything Rafe was even more devastatingly—sinfully!—handsome than he had been eight years ago. He was well over six feet tall, his dark hair was brushed back from his face, the natural swarthiness of the skin he had inherited from his Spanish father adding density to those mesmerizing sky-blue eyes set in a ruggedly chiselled face. His long aquiline nose and curved lips were set above a square jaw that had what most women called either a cleft or a dimple in its centre—but all agreed was sexy as hell. And the black polo shirt and faded denims he wore emphasized the muscled width of his shoulders, tapered waist and lean powerful thighs above long, long legs.

Cairo shook her head. All of this was very well, but none of it explained what he was doing here, taking luggage from the boot of his car! 'What do you think you're doing?'

He straightened. 'Moving in, of course. Grab

a bag, hmm, Cairo?' He slung the bag containing his laptop over his shoulder and picked up the two small suitcases, leaving only a holdall sitting on the driveway.

'Grab a—? Rafe, you can't just— What do you mean, you're *moving in*?' she repeated incredulously.

'Exactly what I said.' He shrugged those broad shoulders as he strode towards her.

Cairo instinctively took a step back. 'I— But— You can't!'

'Why can't I?' he asked calmly.

'Because—because—'

'Stop babbling, Cairo, and bring the bag in.' He didn't so much as pause in those long strides that were rapidly taking him towards the villa.

Towards Cairo's haven of tranquillity after months, years, of never knowing a moment's peace. A peace that Rafe Montero had destroyed the moment he got out of his car!

She hurried to catch up with him and then struggled to match her strides to his much longer ones. 'Rafe, what are you doing here?'

'I could ask you the same question,' he countered without so much as glancing at her. 'Where are Margo and Jeff?'

'They aren't here,' she replied.

Although Cairo was beginning to wish they were—her sister and her husband might have some explanation as to what Rafe Montero was doing here at their holiday villa!

'No?' He arched those dark brows again. 'Have they gone out for the day or just shopping locally?'

'Neither.' Cairo shook her head exasperatedly. 'Rafe, will you just stop and tell me what's going on?' Her voice rose in agitation as she came to a halt, her hands clenched tightly in frustration on the narrowness of her hips.

Rafe slowly placed his luggage inside the front door of the villa before pushing his sunglasses up into his hair once more to look across at Cairo through narrowed lids as he tried to come to terms with her being here.

It had been eight years since he had last seen this woman.

Eight long years.

It was a hell of a shock to suddenly find himself face to face with her again after all that time—

A shock?

Dammit, he was still reeling!

If anything, Cairo Vaughn was even more beautiful. Perhaps a little too thin, he allowed with a slight frown, those almost six feet of curves very willowy now. But her hair was still that long tumbling red, and her legs were still long and shapely beneath the black thigh-length T-shirt. Her face was thinner, too, emphasizing the delicate curve of high cheekbones beneath chocolate-brown eyes, her nose small and straight, but her lips were as full and pouting above the stubborn set of her small, pointed chin as they'd ever been.

Although her cheeks were healthily flushed with temper at the moment, those chocolate-brown eyes looking ready to shoot flames! It made her look more like the famous actress she was than the pale woman whose photograph had been on the front page of the newspapers for months during her very public divorce.

It was none of his business, Rafe told himself

grimly. Just as Cairo herself was none of his business, either.

'So where are Margo and Jeff?' he asked again. He had a few things he would like to say to the other couple concerning the fact that neither of them had warned him that Cairo was going to be here!

'I told you, they aren't here,' Cairo repeated exasperatedly.

Rafe's eyes narrowed. 'At all?'

She shook her head. 'Margo's doctor has ordered complete bed-rest for the last four weeks of her pregnancy.'

Margo and Jeff weren't here.

Only Cairo was.

And neither Margo nor Jeff had bothered to let him know that little fact!

What was he supposed to—?

'Uncle Rafe! Uncle Rafe!'

Rafe just managed to turn in time to catch the small golden-haired bundle dressed in a pink bathing costume as she came hurtling out of the villa and launched herself in his general direction.

Daisy.

Margo and Jeff's six-year-old daughter.

If Cairo had brought Daisy with her, that probably meant she didn't have a lover with her, as well. *Probably…*

'Mummy said you'd be arriving today!' Daisy beamed at him excitedly even as he swung her up to hold her in his arms.

To Cairo only one part of Daisy's statement was relevant. 'Margo *knew* you were coming here?'

'Of course,' Rafe confirmed as he moved Daisy into the crook of one arm to look across at Cairo with guarded blue eyes.

Cairo could barely breathe. Could barely think.

After the last stressful weeks, months, she had desperately needed to get completely away for a while, to be somewhere where she wasn't being constantly photographed wherever she went. Which was why she had been only too happy to accept the suggestion her sister Margo had made, when she'd pointed out that as she and Jeff were unable to go on their usual May holiday to the South of France this year,

Cairo might like to make use of the villa in their stead.

It had been Cairo's own idea, with Margo eight months into what was turning out to be a precarious second pregnancy, that as six-year-old Daisy was on half-term holiday anyway, she could take the little girl with her.

It had all gone so smoothly until now, too. None of the press that had hounded Cairo so doggedly the last ten months had been looking for a woman travelling with a little girl of six. Neither had they recognized the actress Cairo Vaughn behind the dark sunglasses and the baseball cap she had worn to hide the fiery length of her hair as she drove onto the train that would take them through the Eurotunnel into France.

It had been a long drive, of course, but the villa, set high in the hills above Grasse, had been a pleasant surprise, a large, sprawling single-storey building that maintained its rusticity at the same time as providing all the amenities they could possibly want, including a huge pool on the lower terrace, and a number of small shops in the local village that would see to their daily needs.

And Daisy had proved a delightful companion, as only a gregarious six-year-old could, as she kept up a constant stream of chatter on the journey here, and then yesterday threw herself into the pool with enthusiasm once they'd finally reached the villa.

In fact, the simplicity of it all had been a wonderful relief to Cairo after so many years of knowing exactly what she would be doing next week, next month, next year!

But never, during any of Cairo's plans to come to France, had Margo so much as mentioned Rafe Montero. In fact, Cairo hadn't even known that her sister and brother-in-law were still friends with him.

She gave a puzzled shake of her head. 'Margo didn't say anything to me about your coming here.'

'If it's any consolation, she didn't say anything to me about your being here, either,' Rafe retorted sharply.

'It isn't,' Cairo assured him impatiently. 'I appreciate that Margo hasn't been too well recently, but—'

'Perhaps it might be better if we continued this conversation later,' Rafe cut in with a pointed glance at Daisy before he turned his blue gaze warningly on Cairo.

A warning Cairo took absolutely no notice of. 'I really feel we should sort this situation out now, Rafe—'

'Your feeling is noted, Cairo,' he acknowledged brusquely.

Noted, and dismissed, Cairo realized indignantly. Had Rafe always been this infuriating? So arrogantly sure of himself and his surroundings that he totally ignored—or just didn't see or hear!—what anyone else wanted?

Probably, Cairo thought wryly. She had just been too naïve eight years ago, too enthralled by him, too much in love with him, to see it.

Well, she wasn't now and she wouldn't let him get away with it.

'And obviously ignored,' she snapped. 'Rafe, I have absolutely no idea what your arrangement was with Margo and Jeff.' But she certainly intended finding out when she telephoned her sister shortly! 'But as they're obviously still in England, there is no way you can expect to continue with your own plans to stay here.'

He quirked dark brows. 'And just where would you suggest I go instead?'

The hardness in his eyes told her she'd do better to hold back on the reply that she really wanted to make. So instead, Cairo replied, 'To a hotel, of course.'

'You really expect me to be able to do that in the week of the Cannes Film Festival?' he taunted.

'I— The Cannes Film Festival?' she repeated slowly.

'It's the reason I'm in France at the moment,' Rafe explained. '*Work of Art* has been put up for several awards.' He shrugged. 'As director, I'm expected to make an appearance.'

The Cannes Film Festival, Cairo berated herself in her head. Of course Rafe's film had been nominated for an award; it had virtually wiped the board at the Oscars earlier in the year.

'But Cannes is miles away,' she said stubbornly.

'So?'

'So there must be a hotel there where you could stay. It would be much more convenient than being all the way out here, anyway,' Cairo reasoned firmly.

Rafe's mouth tightened. 'I'm sure it's very kind of you to attempt to rearrange my plans for me in this way, Cairo,' he bit out sarcastically. 'But I've been travelling for hours now, and certainly have no intention of discussing this any further until I've at least taken a swim. What do you say, Daisy-May, shall the two of us go for a swim?' He smiled affectionately at the little girl as she gave an excited squeal of approval. 'It would appear you're outnumbered and outgunned, Cairo,' Rafe drawled as he put Daisy down on the tarmacked drive and she instantly took hold of his hand to begin pulling him down towards the swimming pool on the lower terrace.

'But—'

'Outnumbered and outgunned,' Rafe repeated softly as he released his hand from Daisy's to begin pulling his polo shirt over his head, revealing a broad golden expanse of naked chest and shoulders.

Cairo's mouth went dry and her breath caught in her throat as she found herself unable to look away from the sight of Rafe slowly peeling the shirt from his body.

Eight years ago, she had been intimately familiar with every hard, muscled, beautiful inch of Rafe's body, from those wide shoulders, across that muscled chest and flat stomach and down to thrusting thighs.

The time since then had only honed that body, with not an ounce of superfluous flesh on his muscled torso. Rafe's dark hair rested rakishly on his shoulders as he looked across at her with challenging blue eyes. He looked every inch a Spanish conquistador with that mocking smile playing about those chiselled lips. He seemed fully aware that he had rendered Cairo momentarily speechless.

The bastard. He had done that on purpose. Had deliberately—

'Rafe!' she gasped as his hand moved with slow deliberation to unfasten the top button of his denims and slowly slide down the zip.

He arched mocking brows. 'Something wrong, Cairo?' he taunted.

Something was very wrong!

Eight years ago, the two of them hadn't exactly parted the best of friends. In fact, the two of them hadn't seen or spoken to each other again in all that time.

But just to look at him now made Cairo feel breathless, her face hot and flushed. No, *all* of her felt hot and flushed as she found herself unable to look away from those unfastened denims and the deep V of dark hair that disappeared beneath them.

She moistened dry lips. 'Daisy, would you pop into the villa and get us some lemonade to drink by the pool?' She gave her niece what she hoped was a reassuring smile; the muscles in her face didn't seem to be working properly!

'You won't be long, Uncle Rafe?' Daisy paused to ask wistfully.

'Two minutes, Daisy-May,' he promised huskily.

There it was again. That gut feeling that something wasn't quite right about this situation.

And Cairo knew exactly what it was!

Uncle Rafe.

Daisy-May.

It was obvious from Rafe's arrival that Margo and Jeff had kept up their friendship with him, but for how long and how well did Daisy know Rafe that the affection between them was so obvious and the little girl addressed him by the honorary title of 'Uncle'?

And only the family and really close friends ever called Daisy by the affectionate Daisy-May…

Admittedly Cairo had lived mainly in America the last eight years, her visits home infrequent to say the least, but still she would have thought that she would at least have had some idea that her sister and brother-in-law had remained such close friends with Rafe all this time.

Rafe could almost see the disagreeable thoughts racing through Cairo's head. She was undoubtedly annoyed with Margo and Jeff for putting her in this position in the first place.

He could only guess as to the other couple's motives for their actions; Margo and Jeff had never made any secret of the fact that they regretted that he and Cairo had parted eight years ago.

That they 'had parted'! Such simple words to describe such a catastrophic event.

Their last meeting had consisted of a pretty one-sided conversation as Cairo had told him their relationship was over, followed three days later by the announcement of her engagement to Lionel Bond.

A marriage that had now also come to an end.

But Margo and Jeff were whistling in the wind if they thought that little fact was going to make any difference to how Rafe and Cairo felt about each other. Although her obvious determination now to see him leave only made Rafe stubbornly want to do the opposite!

'Lemonade, Cairo?' he commented with a grimace. 'My own preference would have been a glass of wine on the terrace while we gazed out at the view down the valley to the bay of Cannes.'

She glared at him. '*We* aren't going to be *gazing out* at anything together, Rafe,' she snapped. 'In fact—'

'I said let's save the explanations until later, Cairo,' he reminded her forcefully. 'For the moment I intend taking a swim with Daisy.' To prove his point he deliberately slid the zip on his denims the rest of the way before slowly pushing the heavy material down his thighs.

And watched as Cairo's eyes widened, and then widened even more as she realized his intent, her protest only dying on her lips as she saw that Rafe actually wore black swimming trunks beneath the jeans he had now completely removed.

But that momentary lapse in her protests had shown that she wasn't as immune to him as she would have him believe, Rafe noted consideringly. Although he had no doubt, as he saw her shoulders straighten with new determination, that if challenged, she would vehemently deny that awareness.

She drew in a deep breath. 'Rafe, how many times do I have to say it? You are *not* staying here!'

'Sure I am,' he came back easily. 'We'll spend the afternoon swimming and sunbathing with Daisy, then later this evening we can all cook dinner together, and then when Daisy is in bed, the two of us can—'

'We can *what*, Rafe?' Cairo cut in sharply, brown eyes glittering in dark warning as she gave an exasperated shake of her head, having thankfully now regrouped after being completely thrown seconds ago when she had believed Rafe was going to strip off to his underpants.

He usually wore the very briefest of underpants, if her memory served her correctly. And she was pretty sure that it did! Not that the swimming trunks were much better, as the thin material clearly outlined every powerful inch of his hips above long, tanned legs.

Her mouth thinned as she looked up and determinedly met his mocking blue gaze. 'I repeat, Rafe, that the two of us are not going to be doing anything together—not later on this evening when Daisy is in bed, or at any other time!'

'Do I take it from that remark that you aren't pleased to see me again, Cairo?' he murmured throatily.

How had he moved so fast? Cairo wondered slightly dazedly as she suddenly found Rafe was standing only inches away from her, so near she could actually see the pores in the skin of his face. So close that she could actually feel the heat of his body, and smell that clean male smell that was totally Rafe: tangy soap, a lightly elusive after-shave, and a pure animal scent that acted on a woman's senses like a drug. On her senses like a—

No!

This man had broken her heart eight years ago. He hadn't just broken it—the womanizing rat had trampled all over it!

Cairo stood her ground as she refused to be intimidated by the close proximity of his near-nakedness, almost eye to eye with him as Rafe was only a couple of inches taller than her own almost six feet. A compatibility in height that had once given them both incredible pleasure as they—

This was *not* the time to remember that compatibility! What she *should* be recalling was that in every other way that mattered they had been totally *in*compatible.

Her mouth tightened. 'I have no idea what gave you the impression I might be— What are you doing?' She flinched her head back sharply when he would have reached out and touched her cheek.

Rafe's gaze narrowed as he saw her purely instinctive response to the move, his hand dropping slowly back to his side. He wondered just what Cairo's eight-year marriage to Lionel Bond had been like to have caused her to flinch in that way at the merest hint of physical contact.

Unless it was just him that she didn't want to touch her…?

It was a definite possibility, Rafe acknowledged grimly. The last time he and Cairo had spoken together she had left him in absolutely no doubt that, although she had enjoyed their relationship while it had lasted, she now had other plans for her life that most certainly did not include him.

Cairo had taken Hollywood by storm when she'd moved there with her movie-producer husband eight years ago, but even so, she and Rafe had never met again until now. Cairo was a member of the partying set that Rafe avoided at all costs.

Rafe stood unmoving now, his gaze steadily holding Cairo's more wary one as he noted other changes in her beside that ethereal slenderness.

Her eyes, those chocolate-brown orbs that could melt a man's soul, were guarded now rather than glowing as they used to do.

There were dark shadows beneath those eyes, too, as if she hadn't slept well for some time. And there were small delicate lines on either side of the fullness of her mouth, as if a smile had been grimly set there far too often and for far too long as a shield to the inner unhappiness she had no intention of allowing anyone to see or even guess at.

A veneer that had been totally exploded when Cairo had first separated from, and then divorced, her very powerful husband.

On the surface, their marriage had seemed idyllic. A myth that Rafe, along with everyone else who had ever seen or read anything about the couple, had totally believed in until their separation ten months ago....

'Let's all just go for that swim, hmm, Cairo, and talk about this later?' he encouraged softly now.

Cairo stepped away from him. 'You're many things, Rafe, but I never thought stupid as being one of them—' She broke off with a frown as Rafe gave her a derisive smile. 'You find something about this situation amusing?' she bit out irritably.

Yes, Cairo was definitely still in possession of that fiery temperament that had once attracted him so strongly and that made her so electrifying to watch on the big screen.

'Only the way you keep insisting that I have to leave.' He shrugged. 'Even if I could manage to find an available hotel room in the middle of the Cannes Film Festival, I wouldn't,' he admitted.

'Why wouldn't you?'

'Firstly, because I much prefer the peace and quiet to be found here—'

'I agree—it *was* quiet and very peaceful!' Cairo gave him a pointed glare, letting him know clearly that he was the reason that was no longer the case. 'Rafe, you must know I have absolutely no intention of letting you stay on here.'

'Ah.'

'What do you mean, "ah"?' she prompted warily.

'The thing is, Cairo, that brings me to the second reason I have no intention of leaving, either now or in the immediate future,' he told her firmly.

'Which is…?' she challenged.

Rafe couldn't help laughing out loud. 'That I'm not the guest here, Cairo—*you* are. This is my villa,' he added dryly when she continued to look at him blankly.

Cairo stared at Rafe unblinkingly.

Rafe was the 'friend' who let Margo and Jeff stay at his villa in the South of France every year?

CHAPTER TWO

No one looking at Cairo's calm expression, as she relaxed in her bikini on a lounger beside the pool, would ever have guessed at the emotions seething inside her.

Except Rafe, of course.

The cause of those seething emotions!

But he was apparently too busy playing with Daisy, in the pool he had dived into immediately after announcing he owned the villa, to even seem aware of Cairo's presence there, too. Other than physically dragging him out of the pool—which, considering Rafe weighed twice as much as she did, was a non-starter—and demanding he leave, Cairo had little choice but to join the two of them down on the lower terrace.

Dark glasses shielded her eyes from prying

eyes, as well as the glare of the sun as she contemplated her options.

Rafe owned this villa in the South of France.

A little fact that Margo had apparently forgotten to mention for the last eight years, seven of which she and Jeff had been coming to stay here for a couple of weeks every spring!

Or perhaps Margo had simply felt it more diplomatic not to mention that the villa belonged to Rafe....

Cairo had absolutely refused to discuss, with anyone, the reason for the end of her relationship with Rafe Montero. In fact, not only had she refused to talk about him, she had also forbidden Margo to talk to her about him, too. Which would, admittedly, have made it extremely difficult for Margo to tell Cairo that she and Jeff had remained friends with him all these years!

However, there was no way she could stay on here now that she knew Rafe owned the villa, so that meant Cairo had two options.

She could either return to England and the publicity, which, although it was nowhere near as unrelenting as it had been in the States, still dogged Cairo's steps every time she so much as stepped out of the apartment she had bought in London and moved into six months ago.

Or alternatively she could find somewhere else for herself and Daisy to stay in this beautiful area of France.

The latter option was the obvious one, of course. For one thing, Daisy was sure to be very disappointed if they had to cut their holiday short. For another, Cairo really didn't want to return to England yet, seeing as she had actually been enjoying this first proper holiday she had taken in years.

Dammit, why had Rafe Montero had to turn up and disturb their tranquillity in this way?

Also, having turned up, and discovered Cairo here instead of Margo and Jeff, what was he *still* doing here? He had to know how awkward this situation was for her. He also had to know that the two of them couldn't remain here alone— apart from Daisy—together!

He just didn't give a damn.

But then, he never had....

Cairo looked across at him from behind her sunglasses, watching the droplets of water glistening on his face and shoulders as he stood up in the deep end of the pool playing a ball game with Daisy, his dark hair wet now and slicked back from his face as he grinned mischievously at the little girl. That ruggedly handsome face had once made Cairo's heartbeat quicken just to look at it...

She turned sharply away, her hands clenching at her sides as she fought back those painful memories.

Here and now was what mattered.

But here and now Cairo felt completely at a loss to know what to do next. Rafe, on the basis that this villa was actually his, was quite rightly refusing to leave, but the logistics of finding another villa for Daisy and herself to move into seemed overwhelming to Cairo.

And this indecisiveness was Rafe's fault, too!

Because Cairo had allowed herself to relax during the last twenty-four hours, to just let herself be, to exist, to let herself revel in the fact that, after years of making films back to back, she had no pressing work pressures for the next two weeks, when she was due to begin rehearsals for the lead in the London play she had agreed to appear in.

Now Rafe, with his unwanted presence here, was forcing her into once again making decisions, when it was the last thing she felt like doing.

She desperately blinked back the tears of frustration. She wouldn't cry. She would not!

So if she wasn't going to be 'sad,' then she would just have to get 'mad'. And Rafe Montero was the obvious person for her to get mad at!

'Are you coming in for a swim or not?' Rafe leant his arms on the side of the pool as he looked across at her.

He had been totally aware of Cairo the last hour or so as she lay so still and silent on a lounger beside the pool, not reading a book or magazine but just staring off into the distance.

She looked even more slender now that she had removed the overlong T-shirt to reveal that she wore only a brief black bikini beneath; there didn't seem to be an ounce of superfluous flesh on those long silky limbs.

Long, silky limbs that had more than once been entwined with his…

'No, I'm not coming in for a swim,' she answered him tersely now. 'Rafe, you must see that we have to talk about—about the awkwardness, of this situation…?'

Yes, of course he knew the two of them had to talk. Dammit, he was no more happy about finding himself practically alone here with Cairo—young Daisy apart—than she obviously was at having him here.

But neither did he think it was a good idea to have Daisy witness an argument between her aunty Cairo and her 'uncle' Rafe, especially when—as it was sure to!—it resulted in the two of them saying things it would be much better for Daisy not to hear.

His mouth thinned. 'Cairo, how does Daisy seem to you?'

'Seem to me?' she repeated with a frowning

glance at the little girl playing at the other end of the pool by throwing a coin into the water before diving in to collect it.

'Dammit, Cairo.' Rafe quickly ascended the steps that led out of the pool. 'How long is it since you've seen or cared about anyone but yourself?' he demanded as he stood beside her to pick up a towel and begin drying his hair.

Cairo gasped at his accusing tone. 'That is totally unfair, Rafe!' It was also totally unfair what his semi-nakedness was doing to her heart-rate as he leisurely dried himself off with the towel!

'Is it?' he challenged grimly as he moved to sit down on the lounger next to hers. 'Tell me what you see when you look at Daisy,' he ordered.

Cairo stared at him rebelliously for several long seconds before turning her attention to her young niece. 'I see…a little girl having fun playing in the pool,' she said.

'Look again, Cairo. Closer,' he insisted as she would have protested.

Cairo bit back her resentment at his arrogant tone as she turned her attention back to Daisy.

Tall for her age, with shoulder-length golden hair and blue eyes, Daisy looked to her like any other healthy, happy six-year-old on holiday.

Or did she…?

Now that Cairo thought about it, before Rafe's arrival earlier, Daisy hadn't been as chatty this last twenty-four hours. Oh, her niece had played in the pool yesterday and, this morning, had helped Cairo prepare their meals, but she had been less gregarious than usual, less spontaneous, less inclined to do anything, and had refused absolutely to go to the local shops with Cairo this morning so that they could restock on food. Cairo had put this uncharacteristic lack of cooperation down to tiredness after their journey, but what if that wasn't the reason?

Cairo turned frowningly back to Rafe. 'You think she's worried about Margo?'

His mouth twisted derisively. 'What do you think?'

Not knowing how much Daisy actually knew about Margo's condition, Cairo wasn't really sure how to answer that question.

Maybe Rafe was right. Maybe Cairo had been too wrapped up in her own problems just recently to give anyone else's a thought. Although she certainly didn't thank Rafe for being the one to point that out—until now she hadn't even known he liked children, let alone understood Daisy's moods.

She sat up on the lounger. 'Perhaps I should sit down with her and calmly explain that Margo just needs to rest for a few weeks because her blood pressure is a little high—'

'And you think a little girl of six will be reassured by that explanation?' Rafe said sarcastically.

Colour warmed Cairo's cheeks at his intended rebuke. 'I think it might be worth a try, yes!'

He scowled. 'If that's the extent of your knowledge of children, perhaps it's as well that you and Bond never had any!'

Cairo gasped incredulously at his scorn, the fact that she had thought exactly the same thing following her separation from Lionel not important at that moment; Rafe certainly hadn't meant it in the same way she did.

'Look at yourself, Cairo.' Rafe's gaze ran over her with scathing dismissal. 'Perfect hair. Perfect skin. Perfect teeth. Too-perfect body. Perfect damned everything! At least you looked human eight years ago; now you just look like every other *perfect* Hollywood actress!'

Cairo felt her cheeks pale at his deliberately insulting tone. It was too much on top of everything else she had gone through the last eight years.

She stood up. 'When I want your opinion, I'll ask for it— Let *go* of me, Rafe!' she instructed between gritted teeth as he reached out to curl long fingers about her wrist.

A too-slender wrist, Rafe decided even as he felt the creamy softness of her skin beneath his fingers, his gaze moving down to her hand now, the long, slender fingers completely bare of rings. Although there was a slightly whiter band of skin on the third finger of her left hand where her wedding ring and that huge rock that Bond had bought her as an engagement ring used to be….

'I don't think so,' he challenged softly, even as his fingers tightened about her wrist.

Dark sunglasses hid the emotion in her eyes, but the pallor of her cheeks and the unhappy curve of her mouth were evidence of her rising anger.

She was angry? After years of deliberately blocking any memory of Cairo from his mind, Rafe had been forced to relive every single one of them during the last hour. It hadn't improved his temper at all.

His mouth compressed into a thin line. 'How's your career, Cairo?'

Her eyes narrowed with suspicion. 'The last time I looked it was just fine, thank you.'

'Really?' Rafe taunted.

'Yes—really!' she grated.

Rafe shrugged. 'You can't live on the publicity of the divorce for ever, you know. At some time in the not too distant future you'll have to get back to work.'

Cairo's palm itched, her free hand actually aching from the effort it took to stop herself from slapping that arrogant smile from Rafe's mockingly curved lips.

He grimaced. 'I'm just trying to be helpful—'

'When I want your advice, I'll ask for it!' Her eyes flashed an unmistakable warning.

He quirked dark brows. 'Which would be never—right?'

'Right!'

'I'm just interested, Cairo. Relocating yourself to London after your separation doesn't exactly seem like a good career move, does it?' Rafe's gaze was fixed on her face.

'Mind your own damned business!'

'Fine.' He released her abruptly to hold his hands up as he stepped away from her.

Cairo glared at him for several more seconds before giving an abrupt nod. 'If you'll excuse me…'

'Running away, Cairo?' Rafe taunted her as she turned away.

Cairo paused to look back at him, her chin raised stubbornly high. 'I believe you said earlier that you would enjoy a glass of white wine…?'

His brows rose. 'And you're about to go and get me one?'

'If it means I get to spend a little less time in

your unpleasant company, yes!' she bit out. 'But, of course, if you've changed your mind—'

'You should know by now that once my mind is made up about something—or someone—then it rarely changes,' he said pointedly.

'Luckily, neither does mine,' she came back just as pointedly.

They continued to look at each other for several long, tense seconds, a battle of wills that was totally matched in intensity, with neither of them willing to back down.

It had always been like this between them, Rafe recalled ruefully. Cairo might only have been a twenty-year-old actress just starting out in her career eight years ago, but even then she'd had a definite mind of her own, had known exactly what she wanted and how to get it. And eight years ago, she had decided she wanted to become the wife of multi-millionaire movie producer Lionel Bond and unashamedly used her relationship with Rafe as a stepping stone to achieving that goal.

He moved to lie back on the lounger as he

looked out over the terraces of orange trees that surrounded the pool. 'White wine sounds good,' he said curtly.

He felt Cairo continue to look at him frowningly for several more seconds before she turned sharply on her heel and continued up the steps to the villa.

Rafe waited until he was sure she had left before turning to look at her, his hands clenching at his sides as he watched that red hair cascading wildly down a back that seemed endless and almost sensuously feline, a bottom smoothly curving in the black bikini, and legs that were long and shapely.

Dammit, even after all this time, after all that had happened between them, Cairo was still one of the most seductively beautiful women Rafe had ever laid eyes—or hands—on.

Not a comfortable realization for a man who made a point of never becoming involved with a woman. Not any more!

He looked across at Daisy playing in the pool. 'Sweetheart, do you want to go inside and get changed now? It'll be time to eat soon.'

'Okay, Uncle Rafe.' Daisy obediently got out of the pool and went inside the villa.

Cairo's movements were agitated as she collected wine from the fridge and glasses from the cupboard, not forgetting to get some more juice for Daisy, too, in case she fancied a drink.

How dared Rafe even presume to offer her advice?

Rafe had callously broken her heart eight years ago, leaving her completely vulnerable to the face-saving offer of Lionel's marriage proposal—

Cairo came to an abrupt halt in the middle of the kitchen, her eyes closing as she swayed dizzily.

It was the first time she had ever admitted, even to herself, that Rafe's actions were the real reason she had married Lionel….

She shook her head as she once again fought back the tears.

No matter what her reasons might or might not have been for marrying Lionel, despite the fact that she hadn't loved him, she had tried to be a good wife to him, had accompanied him to numerous parties and premieres, always the glamorous and smiling asset. Her work schedule had also been horrendous in recent years, more often than not for Lionel's own production company.

Yes, she really had tried to be the 'perfect' wife to Lionel.

The fact that she had ultimately failed still haunted her….

'Cairo, exactly what are you doing?'

Cairo was so startled by the harsh sound of Rafe's voice behind her that she dropped the carton of juice she was holding, staring down as it seemed to fall in slow motion before landing with a very liquid splat on the tiled floor to spray the juice high into the air.

She gasped as most of that cold juice landed on her bare legs, stepping back quickly, only to come up against a hard, immovable object.

Rafe's body…

Cairo froze as her back came into contact with the searing heat of Rafe's bare chest and thighs, her spine stiffening as she immediately tried to move away from that contact.

It was too much, Rafe decided grimly.

Having an almost naked Cairo pressed against him, her bottom nestled neatly against his hardening thighs, was just too much on top of coming face to face with her again so unexpectedly earlier on.

He grasped her arms to turn her round to face him, knowing by her sudden gasp, the widening of those dark brown eyes as she looked up at him, that she had read the intent in his eyes.

That she knew Rafe was going to kiss her.

Not gently.

Not searchingly.

Certainly not with the slow sensuality with which they used to kiss.

Rafe was hungry.

Very hungry.

So damned hungry for the taste and feel of Cairo that he wanted to strip those two scraps of material from her body, push her against the wall, and take her where she stood!

He held her gaze with his as his arms moved about her like steel bands, moulding her willowy curves against the lean length of his own body before moving his eyes down to look at the parted softness of her lips.

Cairo had always had the most erotic mouth he had ever seen, her lips full and pouting, slightly moistened now, as if inviting and ready for his kiss.

And he was more than ready to kiss her!

Cairo was held mesmerized by the fierceness of Rafe's gaze, but her breath stopped completely as his head swooped and his mouth forcefully claimed hers, deeply, fiercely, demanding a response from her rather than asking for one.

A response Cairo was unable to deny him as her lips seemed to part of their own volition. Her arms moved up and her hands clung to those wide, powerful shoulders, Rafe's skin feeling like steel encased in satin beneath her fingertips.

Heat exploded between them, a fierce, burning heat.

Everywhere were licking flames of complete awareness, of fierce arousal, as her body curved more intimately against Rafe's and she returned the hunger of his kiss.

It had been so long—too long!—since Cairo had felt so stingingly, vibrantly alive!

Rafe's hands, his large, evocative hands, moved caressingly across her back as that devouring kiss continued, Rafe's tongue now thrusting into the moist heat of her mouth, and all the time those hands seeming to burn as they caressed her from hip to breast in restless demand.

Muscles rippled along Rafe's spine as Cairo touched him there, his silky skin feeling hot, hard, and so wonderful.

Cairo was so lost to reason, so totally aroused, that she offered no protest as she felt Rafe unfastening the single hook at the back of her top before one of his hands moved round unerringly to cup the nakedness of her breast.

Cairo melted completely as the soft pad of his thumb moved caressingly across the thrusting pout of her nipple, rivers of pleasure engulfing her—

'Uncle Rafe…?'

Cairo barely had time to register Daisy's presence in the kitchen before Rafe pulled sharply away from her, eyes darkly—briefly—

accusing as he thrust Cairo impatiently behind him before turning to face the little girl.

Rafe breathed raggedly. 'Aunty Cairo and I were just—'

'It's okay, Uncle Rafe, Mummy and Daddy kiss each other all the time,' Daisy told him in that patronizing tone of voice that only a precocious six-year-old could possibly use when talking to an adult. ''Course I didn't know that you and Aunty Cairo kissed, too, but I suppose it's all right.' She shrugged.

'That's very—adult, of you, Daisy,' Rafe told her dryly.

'Grown-ups are always kissing and stuff,' Daisy assured him with a total lack of interest.

Cairo was hastily dealing with her bikini top—not having as much luck fastening it as Rafe had done unfastening it because her fingers trembled so much!—but even so she was aware of the muscles rippling in Rafe's back as he suppressed a chuckle at Daisy's bored dismissal of the scene she had just witnessed.

Cairo certainly didn't share his humour concerning this totally embarrassing situation. Rafe had only been back in her life a matter of hours and already she was allowing him to kiss her!

Well…no, she hadn't exactly allowed him to kiss her—being Rafe he had just taken the opportunity to kiss her.

And he wasn't 'back in her life', either—something she intended making very plain to him the next time they were alone together.

So far today Rafe had mocked her, taunted her and insulted her—he certainly wasn't going to get away with making love to her whenever he felt like it!

Cairo drew in a controlling breath as she stepped out from behind Rafe, her bikini top now firmly back in place. 'What would you like to do first, Daisy, cook dinner or phone Mummy?'

Daisy's face instantly brightened. 'Phone Mummy!'

'We'll go and do it right now,' Cairo promised, determinedly keeping her gaze averted from Rafe's as she crossed the kitchen to take the excited Daisy's hand in her own.

'Don't worry about me,' Rafe drawled behind them. 'I'll just stay here and clear up this sticky juice from the floor, shall I?'

Cairo turned back to give him a mocking smile. 'That's very kind of you, Rafe,' she accepted lightly. 'I'm sure you'll find everything you need in the cupboard under the sink,' she added.

His eyes glittered dangerously. 'Not everything that I need, Cairo,' he ground out harshly.

She gave him a censorious frown. 'Just do your best, hmm?' she snapped.

'I usually do,' he stated deliberately.

Cairo shot him a silencing glare before leaving the kitchen, Daisy's hand still tucked trustingly in her own.

CHAPTER THREE

RAFE had showered, dressed, already had the barbecue alight and ready for cooking the steaks for their dinner, and was sitting on the terrace drinking another glass of white wine by the time Cairo and Daisy rejoined him outside. Daisy looked very cute in her blue corduroy skirt and pink T-shirt, and Cairo looked even better in flat sandals, her tanned legs bare, and a dark green, knee-length, strappy silk dress that clung in all the right places.

Or—depending on your point of view—all the wrong ones, Rafe allowed wryly as his gaze lingered on the bareness of her tanned shoulders and the tops of her breasts.

It had been a mistake to kiss Cairo earlier, he acknowledged now. But it was simply the most recent of the many mistakes he had made where she was concerned—allowing himself to fall for her eight years ago having definitely been the worst one of them all....

His mouth tightened as he raised his gaze to hers. 'Help yourself to a glass of wine,' he invited as she moved to sit down at the other end of the marble-topped dining table. 'How was Margo?'

'Very well,' Cairo answered distantly as she poured some of the white wine into a second glass—and having absolutely no intention of telling him what her sister's reply had been when Cairo had challenged her over Rafe's arrival earlier today.

'Get over yourself!' had been Margo's unhelpful comment.

It wasn't herself Cairo had to get over—it was Rafe's mockery of her and her resentment towards him!

'It's high time the two of you got over that, too,' had been Margo's response to that claim.

Not exactly helpful advice when even now

Cairo could feel the antagonism between Rafe and herself burning beneath the surface of this polite exchange.

Not that Rafe looked particularly concerned by it. In fact, he looked altogether too disturbingly handsome in faded denims and an open-necked, short-sleeved shirt the same shade of blue as his eyes, the dampness of his hair brushed back from those hard, aristocratically chiselled features inherited from his Spanish father.

Cairo had chosen her own dress for this evening with care, knowing she would need all her self-confidence to face Rafe again after that heated exchange in the kitchen. She had also swept her hair up and secured it loosely on her crown, leaving her neck and shoulders bare, her face already lightly tanned and requiring only a peach gloss applied to her lips.

The lips that still felt tinglingly sensitive and slightly bruised from the force of Rafe's kiss!

'Mummy said to say hello, Uncle Rafe,' Daisy told him happily.

'Did she, now?' he drawled.

'Yes.' The little girl nodded. 'And she hopes you do well at the film festival.'

'That's very thoughtful of her,' Rafe accepted dryly—he had a few things he intended saying personally to Margo once Daisy was safely tucked up in bed! 'Can your aunty Cairo make a salad, do you think?' he teased gently as he stood up to turn the steaks on the barbecue.

Daisy gave a giggle. 'Aunty Cairo cooked omelettes last night.'

'Did she now?' Rafe quirked dark, mocking brows. 'She's obviously a woman of many talents!' he added with a taunting sideways glance at 'Aunty Cairo'.

Daisy seemed completely unaware of the intended insult to her aunt, singing quietly to herself as she began to lay the table outside for the three of them.

But Cairo certainly wasn't, the narrow-eyed glare she gave Rafe letting him know in no uncertain terms that she wasn't amused.

Rafe returned Cairo's look for several long seconds, his smile derisive, before he turned his full attention to cooking the steaks. The problem was that Cairo was just too beautiful for him—or any other man!—to look at for too long without wanting to take her to bed.

Which was something that was never going to happen ever again, Rafe told himself grimly, in spite of the fact that he had enjoyed kissing her earlier. No, he'd more than enjoyed it—he had been wanting to repeat the experience ever since.

Eight years, dammit—and within hours of seeing her again Rafe's body ached with the desire that had been aroused earlier and remained unfulfilled!

'How is Margo, really?' he asked once Daisy had gone into the kitchen to collect the cutlery.

Cairo shrugged those delectably bare shoulders. 'She believes that the specialist is thinking of admitting her to the clinic tomorrow if her blood pressure hasn't gone down by then.'

Rafe could hear the underlying concern in Cairo's voice. 'She wasn't ill like this with Daisy, was she?'

'Not as far as I'm aware, no.' Cairo frowned.

'I haven't spent a great deal of time in England the last few years, Rafe,' she explained sharply as he raised questioning brows.

His lip curled scornfully. 'Too busy making a name for yourself in Hollywood, I expect.'

'That's where Lionel lived, Rafe,' she said defensively as she heard the censure in his tone. 'And where he worked. It was only natural that I should mainly work there, too.'

Really, this man seemed to think that everything she did, everything she said, was suspect— especially if it allowed him to make some cutting comment about it!

'I seem to remember that you once said your main love was the stage,' he said huskily. 'I even talked of moving to England for a while so that I could be with you when you accepted the part you had been offered in *The Graduate*.'

Cairo gave a pained frown. Yes, Rafe had talked of staying temporarily in England. But that had been before he'd become bored with their relationship and had an affair with another woman!

Her mouth tightened. 'So you could be with me *and* all those other adoring females panting at your bedroom door!' she dismissed scathingly. 'If you'll excuse me, Rafe,' she added, standing up abruptly, 'I need to go and make the salad.'

Dinner hadn't exactly been a relaxed meal, Cairo acknowledged ruefully as they cleared everything away a couple of hours later. Thankfully Daisy, reassured after her earlier chat on the telephone with her mother, was back to her normal, talkative self, and her chatter had filled in the silence that had existed between Rafe and Cairo. The two of them had barely addressed a word directly to one another—'could you please pass the salt?' really didn't count as conversation!

Rafe excused himself to make a telephone call while Cairo put Daisy to bed, delaying as long as she possibly could in her niece's bedroom before rejoining Rafe on the terrace. She finally came outside to find him watching the last rays of sunset gleaming redly in the rapidly darkening sky, dozens of lights on in the houses dotted in the valley below.

Cairo stood hesitantly in the doorway, not altogether comfortable with the air of intimacy that surrounded him.

'Sit down, Cairo,' he ordered without turning.

She gasped. 'How did you—?'

'Your perfume,' he elaborated as he turned to look at her. 'Stop hovering over there in the doorway, Cairo, and come and sit down.'

Her eyes widened indignantly at his autocratic tone. 'You always were arrogant, Rafe. I'm sure that as a director you wield a lot of authority, but I can assure you—'

'For God's sake, *sit down*, Cairo!' He turned to look at her, blue eyes glittering brightly in the semi-darkness. 'I want to talk to you about Margo,' he added impatiently as she remained unmoving in the doorway.

'Oh. Fine.' She moved to sit in the chair furthest away from his own. 'That's who you were talking to on the telephone just now?'

'It's good to know that all those years of

marriage to Lionel Bond didn't completely dull your intelligence!'

'Rafe—'

'Will you just shut up and listen for once, Cairo?' He stood up to move restlessly to the edge of the terrace. 'I spoke to Jeff, as it happens. Apparently Margo, for obvious reasons, was deliberately keeping the situation light when she spoke to you and Daisy earlier.' His expression was grim. 'They're concerned about the baby now, as well as Margo, and the doctor's intention is to admit her tomorrow and perform a Caesarian section.'

Cairo stood up abruptly. 'I'll make arrangements for myself and Daisy to return home immediately—'

'That's the last thing Jeff wants you to do!' Rafe turned to her swiftly. 'Cairo, he has no idea how the operation is going to turn out, for either Margo or the baby, and the last thing he wants is for Daisy to go back to England and get caught up in the middle of that uncertainty. Even if the operation is a success, Margo and the baby will have to stay in hospital for several days, so there'll be plenty of time then for you to arrange to get back for her homecoming.'

'Even if the operation is a success' was the only thing in Rafe's last statement that registered with Cairo....

She swallowed hard. 'Is there— What do they think the chances are of them both being okay?'

Rafe wasn't enjoying this conversation at all. He knew that the two sisters, having lost both parents in a car accident ten years ago, had remained emotionally close, even though they had lived on different continents for years. It was because of the sisters' closeness that Rafe had got to know Margo and Jeff in the first place....

'Cairo—'

'Just answer me, will you, please, Rafe?' she said tautly, her eyes gleaming brightly with unshed tears, her hands clenched at her sides as she faced him tensely.

Under other circumstances—with any other woman—Rafe knew he would have taken her in his arms and comforted her. But after what had happened between the two of them earlier, Rafe didn't dare touch Cairo again!

Instead he remained where he was, several feet away, his expression remote. 'Jeff believes there's a good chance that both Margo and the baby will be fine—'

'Thank God!' Cairo breathed her relief, some of the tension relaxing in her shoulders. 'But…?' she added shrewdly, as if she sensed that Rafe hadn't told her everything Jeff had said.

Rafe grimaced at her perception. 'He also asked if the two of us would remain here with Daisy until he knows exactly what's happening.' And if Cairo thought he was any happier about that request than she was, then she was completely mistaken! 'The idea being that, between the two of us, we keep Daisy so busy, at least over the next couple of days, that she doesn't have too much time to telephone or think too much about what's going on at home.'

Cairo blinked. 'Jeff wants the two of us to stay on here *together*?' she repeated incredulously.

Rafe's mouth tightened at her tone. 'I can be civilized about this if you can, Cairo.'

As far as Cairo was concerned it wasn't a question of either of them being 'civilized'. She had been hoping, once Daisy was in bed, that she and Rafe could finally have a sensible conversation about one of them leaving. Preferably Rafe. And preferably this evening!

But Jeff's request had quashed that idea and instead her brother-in-law was asking her to stay on here with Rafe. Well, obviously not just with Rafe—if Daisy weren't here, then Jeff wouldn't have needed to make the request in the first place.

Cairo knew perfectly well it would be Rafe who would be the dominant presence over the next couple of days; it was obvious the two of them couldn't even be in the same country without arguing.

As indicated by this conversation alone!

But at the same time she recognized that Jeff did have a point; after only a few hours Cairo could see the rapport between Rafe and Daisy, and that being with him had already lightened the little girl's introspective mood. That those same few hours had been absolute purgatory for Cairo really shouldn't come into the equation when it was Daisy's peace of mind they were all concerned about.

Nevertheless…

She frowned. 'Do you actually have to stay here at the villa for us to do that?'

'*I* own it, Cairo!' Rafe reminded her irritably.

She shrugged. 'Then maybe I should be the one to move to a hotel—'

'Will you stop being so childish!' Rafe interrupted forcefully. 'Or is it just that you don't trust yourself to be alone here with me even for a couple of days?' he jeered.

Her eyes glittered with anger as she instantly responded with all the sarcasm of which she was capable. 'Don't flatter yourself, Rafe!'

'Oh, yeah, I forgot.' His mouth twisted with distaste. 'You've had so many lovers the last few years you were probably looking forward to a break for a few weeks!'

'I didn't have any lovers during my marriage!' Cairo protested vehemently.

He shrugged. 'That wasn't what Bond said ten months ago.'

'He was angry at the time, making things up,' Cairo defended herself a little shakily.

'Sure he was—'

'Don't use that patronizing tone with me, Rafe!' she blazed at him. 'I did *not* have an affair during my marriage to Lionel!'

Rafe's brows rose. 'Aren't you protesting a little too much, Cairo?' he taunted softly.

She shook her head. 'I'm merely trying to explain that Lionel was upset when he made those accusations, because I had left him.' Her chin rose. 'Besides, your own numerous relationships over the years haven't exactly been a well-kept secret!' she challenged.

As his clandestine relationship eight years ago with his co-star Pamela Raines hadn't remained the secret he had hoped, either...

'The difference being that I'm not married,' he pointed out.

'No, you've never made that commitment, have you, Rafe?' she scorned.

'Not if it meant I was ultimately going to end up with an unfaithful wife like you, no,' he rasped.

'Haven't you been listening to a word I've said?'

'Oh, I listened, Cairo,' he snarled. 'I just have great difficulty believing your claim of innocence!'

Cairo swallowed hard. 'You take delight in insulting me, don't you, Rafe?'

No, dammit, Rafe didn't take any delight in talking about the other men Lionel Bond had claimed Cairo had been involved with during their marriage. As far as he was concerned, if the glitter to her marriage had worn off, if Cairo had been unhappy with Bond—and it now appeared that she had been—then she should have just got out, not taken a string of lovers to compensate for that unhappiness.

Rafe's mouth thinned. 'Our being here isn't about you or me, Cairo,' he growled. 'This is about a six-year-old little girl that we need to keep distracted so that Jeff can feel free to concentrate on Margo and the baby.'

He was right. Cairo knew he was right. Rafe had just shaken her by talking of the things

Lionel had said in anger when she'd told him she was leaving him, accusations he had later privately apologized for. Too late, of course, for the press had already gleefully printed the lies and were not inclined to print a retraction.

It was also disconcerting to realize that Rafe's affection for her niece was such that he was even willing to stay on here with Cairo when he would obviously rather not. Cairo had never thought of Rafe as being in the least paternal, and yet his obvious feelings for Daisy clearly disproved that….

Again posing the question as to why Rafe had never married and had children of his own. Today had at least shown Cairo that he would make a wonderful father.

It was his role as a faithful husband that would be in question!

'You're right,' she admitted. 'I'm willing to— to try and put our differences aside, if you are.'

Rafe's teeth gleamed whitely in the darkness as he gave a humourless smile. 'Call a truce, you mean?'

'Call a halt to the insults and accusations, I mean,' Cairo told him determinedly.

He shrugged. 'I'll behave if you will.'

'Then we're agreed. For Daisy's sake, we will try to give every outward appearance of getting on together for at least the next two days.'

Rafe inclined his head in acquiescence. 'For Daisy's sake.'

Cairo hesitated in the doorway. 'And there will be no repeat of—of what happened in the kitchen earlier,' she added huskily, still not completely reconciled inside herself to how easily—how fiercely!—she had responded when Rafe had taken her in his arms earlier and kissed her.

No doubt a lot of soul-searching was in order once she reached the privacy of her bedroom!

'Ah. Now that's something else, Cairo.' Rafe folded his arms across the width of his chest as he regarded her with mocking eyes. 'After all, it may just turn out that you can't keep your hands off me.'

'In your dreams, Rafe,' she scoffed.

'Maybe. We'll see, won't we...'

No, they would not 'see', Cairo determined as

she stormed off, making her way to her bedroom at the front of the house.

A couple of days, that was all this was going to be. And surely she could avoid finding herself in any compromising situations with Rafe for that short length of time?

CHAPTER FOUR

'Don't forget your mobile phone— Cairo, what the hell are you wearing?'

Cairo, about to push her sunglasses up onto the bridge of her nose, instead paused in the movement to look at Rafe over the top of them as he stared at her with a scowl on his face.

She knew it wasn't the sunglasses he was referring to, or the white T-shirt and skirt she was wearing with flat sandals, so that left…

'A baseball cap, of course,' she snapped dismissively as she adjusted the peak of the white cap further down her forehead, her hair gathered up and looped through the fastening at the back to hang down in a loose ponytail. 'An item of headgear that originated in your mother's country, I believe,' she added dryly.

'So did the Stetson, but that doesn't mean I'd ever wear one,' Rafe retorted.

The three of them had spent most of the morning down by the pool until Rafe had suggested a trip out to collect more food supplies from the local supermarket. Daisy had then added her own idea that after they had brought the food back to the villa they could all go down into Grasse and have lunch in one of the many restaurants there before going on to one of the beaches along the coast.

A suggestion Rafe said he was more than happy to go along with, and meaning that Cairo was once again 'outgunned and outnumbered'!

But that didn't mean she was willing to go out without the disguise of her baseball cap. 'I tend to freckle in the direct sun,' she explained mendaciously.

His mouth quirked. 'And we mustn't let a freckle ruin that perfect complexion, must we?'

Her eyes narrowed. 'Rafe, why don't you—'

'Actually, Uncle Rafe, Aunty Cairo is famous,' Daisy informed him airily. 'She wears

the hat because she doesn't want people to rec-
ognize— I'm sorry, Uncle Rafe, I didn't hear
what you said…?'

Daisy might not have been able to discern
Rafe's mumbled response, but Cairo certainly
had, and she didn't appreciate his comment of
'*infamous* more aptly describes it'!

'I'm nowhere near as famous as your uncle
Rafe, Daisy,' she assured the little girl lightly
even as she shot Rafe a quelling glance before ad-
justing the sunglasses onto the bridge of her nose.

And completely hiding the expression in those
dark brown eyes, Rafe noted—although it wasn't
too difficult to imagine what it was!

'Come on, Daisy-May.' He ruffled the little girl's
golden curls. 'We'll wait outside in the car while
your aunty Cairo finishes putting on her disguise.'

'Very funny, Rafe,' Cairo drawled as she fell
into step beside them. 'Make sure you bring a
bag out with you later, Daisy—your uncle is
something of a sex-symbol, and we may need to
beat off his female fans before the day is out,' she
warned her niece conspiratorially.

'Now who's being funny?' Rafe raised dark brows as he opened the back door of the car so that Daisy could climb inside.

Cairo gave him a sweetly mocking smile. 'I'm only stating the obvious, Rafe,' she jeered.

Rafe grimaced. 'A sex-symbol?'

She shrugged narrow shoulders as she moved round to the passenger side of the car. 'I seem to remember reading somewhere that you were voted the sexiest man in America last year.'

Not a title he was particularly proud of.

As, no doubt, Cairo was well aware!

'I'm surprised, with all that was going on in your own life this last year, that you could find the time to read about mine, as well,' he jibed.

The teasing smile faded from her lips. 'It made a pleassant change from some of the other trash that was being printed at the time!'

Rafe quickly moved round the car to where she stood. 'Cairo—'

'We really should be going, Rafe,' she told him brittlely as she opened the car door herself to get inside and close the door firmly behind her.

Leaving Rafe standing in the driveway feeling like a heel. They had called a truce last night, for Daisy's sake, and for most of the morning he had kept to that truce, as had Cairo. His present lapse was due, he knew, to the fact that he hadn't slept at all well last night and that lack of sleep was catching up with him.

But how could he sleep when he knew that Cairo was in another bed just down the hallway? Probably as awake as he was, if for different reasons.

He hadn't been able to forget how good Cairo had felt when he'd touched her earlier, but Cairo would have been worrying about Margo, something Rafe knew he hadn't taken too much into consideration during their conversation. But hell, at the time Jeff had just asked him to stay on here and take care of Cairo and Daisy. A request, for Daisy's sake, Rafe had known he couldn't refuse.

But that didn't mean he had to like being here with Cairo.

Any more than Cairo had to like being here with him, perhaps?

'I'm sorry,' Rafe muttered as he got in the car beside her and switched on the engine.

Cairo gave him a startled look. 'What?'

Rafe drew in a sharp breath. 'I said I'm sorry,' he repeated more clearly. 'It was a cheap shot.'

'Yes, it was,' she agreed huskily—although an apology was the last thing she had been expecting!

He gave a wry smile. 'I guess I deserved that.'

'I guess you did.' She nodded.

Rafe scowled. 'Were you always this—opinionated?'

'Probably not,' she conceded softly. 'I guess time changes all of us. And not always for the better.' She shrugged.

Cairo knew she had changed over the last eight years, that her life with Lionel had brought about subtle if not major differences in her. For instance, she no longer trusted even affection, let alone rakishly attractive men like Rafe Montero!

Rafe gave Cairo several sideways glances as he drove them down into the village, Daisy exclaiming in the back of the car as she pointed out several of her favourite haunts from previous holidays taken here.

At one time, Cairo would have been almost as happy as Daisy was by a trip to the shops and then into town for lunch. But not now, Rafe realized. It wasn't so much that she had grown cynical as that her emotions were hidden away behind a wall of indifference that seemed almost impenetrable.

Or perhaps she was just bored, Rafe conceded ruefully. After all, this holiday with a six-year-old was probably a bit tame for her after the exotic life she'd led in Hollywood with Lionel Bond.

The sort of life Rafe avoided for the main part.

Oh, he couldn't escape attending some of the parties or award ceremonies—like the one in Cannes this week. But given a choice Rafe preferred to be at his house on the beach, well away from the falseness and artificiality of the majority of the social scene in Hollywood itself.

But it was a life that Cairo, photographed at numerous glitzy parties over the years, had obviously thoroughly enjoyed.

'How about we go to St Moritz for lunch instead of Grasse?' he suggested once they had finished shopping in the local supermarket and were waiting beside the car for Daisy to come back from returning the trolley.

'St Moritz?' Cairo echoed guardedly.

He nodded. 'We can either drive down the coast or get a boat across from—'

'I know how to get there, Rafe, I've been there before,' she cut in before shaking her head. 'I just don't see the appeal for a six-year-old girl.'

Of course she had been there before, Rafe acknowledged self-derisively. No doubt Cairo had been to all the fashionable in-places during her marriage, which meant she probably wouldn't be interested in a trip to the sophistication of Monte Carlo, either, which was down the coast from Cannes in the opposite direction from St Mortiz.

So much for Rafe's decision to try to make up for being so awful to her earlier on today.

'I just thought a twenty-eight-year-old woman might be missing the shops on Rodeo Drive!' he drawled.

Delicate colour warmed Cairo's cheeks at the deliberate taunt. Shortly after her arrival in Los Angeles Lionel had opened accounts for her in all the exclusive stores on Rodeo Drive, and Cairo had to admit that for the first few months of their marriage it had been fun to go into any of those shops and buy anything that caught her eye.

But the novelty of shopping, like the gloss of her already failing marriage, had soon worn off, and she had been relieved to get back to work.

'I don't miss anything about my life in Los Angeles,' she told Rafe flatly.

'Nothing?' he scorned.

'Absolutely nothing,' she echoed coldly.

'I find that very hard to believe,' he commented. 'I seem to recall that never a week went by when your photograph didn't appear in the newspapers or some glossy magazine as one of the "beautiful people" attending some party or premiere.'

'Which I hated,' Cairo told him stiffly. 'It was Lionel's way of life, not mine,' she added as Rafe raised sceptical brows.

'No?'

he hadn't lived like a monk the last eight years, and those years had fooled him into believing himself well over her. But since he had kissed and caressed her yesterday afternoon in the kitchen he knew that he wasn't over her at all.

There was no doubt Cairo was different now, sleekly so, her clothes all designer-label, everything about her more sophisticated and self-assured than the bright-eyed twenty-year old he had met while filming on the Isle of Man.

But he would be lying if he claimed that the attraction, that fierce ache to make love with her, wasn't still burning beneath their thin veneer of civility.

Extremely dangerous.

And it was a danger Rafe needed to get away from, if only for a few hours!

'For obvious reasons I have to go down into Cannes this evening,' he told Cairo as the two of them put the shopping away while Daisy collected her swimming things from her bedroom.

'Fine,' Cairo accepted without interest as she continued to put cereals away in a cupboard.

'You and Daisy can come with me if you like?' Rafe heard himself offer—in complete contradiction to his thoughts of a few minutes ago…

His only excuse was that Cairo's complete lack of interest in his plans for this evening had annoyed the hell out of him!

Cairo stiffened before slowly turning to face Rafe. 'Why on earth would I want to do that?' she prompted incredulously while inwardly shying away from the thought of going anywhere near all that glitzy artificiality again after she had so enjoyed avoiding it the last ten months.

As Rafe had pointed out earlier, she had attended numerous award ceremonies with Lionel over the years, both as an actress in her own right and as Lionel's wife, had even been nominated for and won an Oscar herself three years ago.

Which meant Cairo knew exactly what the party in Cannes this evening would be like, everyone really there to see and be seen rather than to actually meet up and chat with old friends and just enjoy themselves.

Rafe leant back against one of the kitchen units

to study her through narrowed lids. 'You haven't worked in almost a year, Cairo.'

She blinked. 'Sorry?'

His mouth thinned. 'You haven't made a film in over ten months.'

'So?'

'So, as I pointed out yesterday, the world of acting is a fickle one.' He shrugged. 'Too long out of the limelight, and the industry, as well as the public, tends to forget you exist.'

'Your point being?'

He frowned. 'My point being, you need to get back to work!'

Cairo gave a humourless laugh. 'As I told you yesterday, I really don't see what business it is of yours—'

'You can't hide away for the rest of your life, Cairo,' he pointed out.

Her eyes widened. 'I'm *not* hiding—'

'What else would you call it?' he attacked her impatiently. 'You're staying in a villa miles from anywhere, and you wear sunglasses and a baseball cap to disguise your appearance when you do go out. I'd call that hiding, wouldn't you, Cairo?'

'No,' she bit out. 'What I would call it is taking a well-earned holiday after years of constantly working my—' She stopped and drew in a controlling breath. 'I can't remember the last time I was able to just relax and lie in the sun.'

'You'll freckle, remember?' he taunted.

'I'll risk it!' she snapped. 'And I really don't see what any of this has to do with my not wanting to come to a party in Cannes with you this evening.'

'There will be directors there. Producers, too. The people who will give you your next job, Cairo,' Rafe explained patiently as she made no response.

'I don't need anyone to give me my next job, Rafe,' she assured him.

He studied her carefully. 'You already know what you're going to work on next, don't you?'

Cairo gave a mocking inclination of her head. 'Yes, Rafe, I already know what I'm going to work on next.'

'Which is?'

'None of your business!'

'Are the two of you arguing?' Daisy asked from the kitchen doorway, her expression curious rather than concerned.

'Of course not, poppet,' Cairo hastened to reassure her. 'Uncle Rafe and I were just—having a discussion about something unimportant.' She shot Rafe a warning glance.

'Oh.' Daisy nodded. 'Because Mummy and Daddy always kiss and make up when they have an argument.'

Cairo snorted at the thought of her and Rafe ever being able to 'kiss and make up'. There was simply too much history between them for them ever to be able to do that!

A sentiment Rafe obviously agreed with as he answered the little girl. 'As Aunty Cairo said, Daisy, we weren't arguing,' he said dryly. 'So, who's hungry?' he added enticingly, Daisy's shout of agreement completely overshadowing the fact that Cairo said nothing.

She was too irritated with Rafe to speak, that was why!

She had spent years being persuaded, cajoled and pushed by Lionel into taking one film role after another, usually for his production company, of course, and she wasn't about to be railroaded by anyone else—least of all the arrogant Rafe Montero—into doing anything, or going anywhere, she didn't want to go.

She certainly wasn't going to allow Rafe to goad her into going to Cannes with him this evening!

But he seemed no more interested in pursuing the subject as they found a place to park in Grasse before walking through to the shops and restaurants. In fact—thankfully!—Rafe seemed decidedly distracted again, leaving Cairo to enjoy the aromas and atmosphere of the town whose main industry was its wonderful perfumes.

Rafe hadn't been being paranoid earlier about the blue car and its driver…

He was pretty sure of it now, the little blue car having come out of a side road as Rafe drove down from the villa and out onto the main road. It had then stayed a two-car distance behind them on the drive to Grasse, and followed them into the same car park once they got into the town. Although the driver, definitely the same man as before, noticing Rafe's narrow-eyed interest across the car park as he got out of the blue car, had quickly locked the doors before disappearing in the opposite direction to the one Rafe, Cairo and Daisy took.

Admittedly Rafe hadn't seen the man since, but a sixth sense, a tingling sensation at the back of his neck, told him that the man was still around somewhere.

Was he just an avid movie fan who had maybe recognized Rafe when he arrived at the supermarket?

Or—worse!—a reporter?

Several people had given Rafe a second glance as the three of them strolled through the busy streets of Grasse, as if they thought they recognized him, only to look at Cairo and Daisy and decide they must be mistaken; Rafe Montero wasn't married, let alone father to a six-year-old girl.

But the man in the blue car seemed more

dogged than that, and he had obviously been waiting at the bottom of the access road in the hopes of being able to follow the next time Rafe left the villa.

Or Cairo did….

Rafe gave her a frowning glance. She was still wearing the baseball cap and dark sunglasses, but otherwise seemed relaxed, and was obviously enjoying herself as she and Daisy looked at scented candles as a present to take home to Margo.

Something Rafe doubted she would continue to be if the man following them should turn out to be a reporter hot on her trail!

'Is everything all right, Rafe?' Cairo queried once the three of them were seated at a shaded table in the square where they had decided to have lunch.

He raised dark brows. 'Why shouldn't it be?'

Cairo frowned. 'You seem—preoccupied, that's all.'

'I get that way when I'm hungry,' he dismissed, before pointedly turning his attention to reading the menu.

Cairo continued to look at him for several more seconds before looking down at her own menu; after all, she had no reason for complaint as long as Rafe continued to help keep Daisy entertained.

Besides, he was probably as worried about Margo as Cairo was.

She had spoken briefly to Jeff on the telephone this morning, her brother-in-law promising to call her later today once he had any news about Margo and the baby. Cairo's mobile was turned on in her shoulder-bag for just that reason.

It was very pleasant sitting here in the sunshine, Cairo decided as she relaxed back in her chair once they had given their order to the waiter and Daisy and Rafe were busy discussing the merits of the beaches in the area, something they were both familiar with if the friendly argument that ensued was anything to go by.

Cairo watched the two of them from behind dark sunglasses, appreciating how good Rafe was with Daisy, talking to her as an adult rather than a child as he considered the merits of her suggestions, Daisy obviously equally enthralled with him.

Again Cairo asked herself why he had never married and had children of his own…

Rafe was thirty-seven now, at the very top of his profession, a successful director, as well as one of the most sought after—and sexy—actors in the world: the most sexy according to that American poll last year!

There had been plenty of women in Rafe's life over the years, too, photographs of him with those beautiful women often appearing in the glossily expensive magazine that she occasionally read while waiting in her trailer to be called on set.

Yet he had never married, had remained one of the most elusively eligible bachelors in the world…whom Cairo knew herself to be completely physically aware of!

It would be futile to claim otherwise when she was sensitive to everything about him, from his silkily dark hair that brushed the collar of his black polo shirt, down to the bareness of his slimly elegant feet casually thrust into black deck-shoes.

He was as sexy as hell, Cairo acknowledged

achingly. Even more so than he had been eight years ago, maturity having added another dimension to his already many-faceted personality, lines of experience now beside the deep blue of his eyes, his rare smile one of mocking challenge.

'She's a great kid, isn't she?' Rafe said as Daisy excused herself to go to the ladies' room inside the restaurant.

'Er—yes, she is,' Cairo agreed abruptly even as she wrenched her gaze away from the moulded perfection of Rafe's sensually curving mouth and her thoughts from the memory of how forcefully that mouth had claimed hers yesterday afternoon.

Rafe's gaze narrowed on her flushed cheeks. 'Have you ever wondered that if we had made it together, we might have had a daughter of Daisy's age by now? Maybe a couple more, too?'

'Certainly not!' she denied firmly.

Rafe shrugged. 'Just a thought.'

Thank goodness she hadn't become pregnant during their three-month affair—that really would have complicated a situation that had ultimately proved heartbreaking enough when Rafe had become bored with her naïve adoration and secretly turned his attentions to another, much more experienced, woman.

But she couldn't deny that at one time, in her naivety, she had inwardly, deliciously thought about becoming the mother of Rafe's children….

'I think I'll just try giving Jeff a call while Daisy isn't here.' She took her mobile from her bag and put the call through to her brother-in-law, effectively putting an end to that conversation.

But if nothing else, it had served as a reminder that Cairo hadn't been enough for Rafe eight years ago, and despite her earlier thoughts of how wonderful he was with Daisy—of what a good father he would make to his own children someday—Cairo knew that she wouldn't be enough for him now, either.

Rafe took advantage of Cairo's preoccupation to sit back and run a lazily sweeping glance over the busy square, aware that he still had that uncomfortable prickling sensation at the base of his nape, as if he was being watched.

Not that he had actually seen the driver of the blue car again.

But perhaps that wasn't surprising after Rafe had shown him so clearly in the car park that he was aware of the other man's interest?

Or maybe Rafe was wrong and it really was co-incidence that he had seen that particular man in that particular car twice in one day?

Maybe…

He just didn't happen to believe that strongly in coincidences—

'Dammit!' Rafe grated harshly even as he surged angrily to his feet and turned to stride towards where he had just seen Daisy emerge from the ladies' room in the restaurant.

To where a man—the same man who had earlier been driving the blue car, Rafe was sure of it—had stopped her and engaged her in conversation!

CHAPTER FIVE

'FOLLOW him, Rafe!' Cairo cried anxiously behind him as the man saw Rafe's approach and quickly broke off his conversation with Daisy to turn on his heel and hurry out through the back entrance of the restaurant.

Rafe didn't need any encouragement—he had every intention of going after the other man.

'Take care of Daisy,' he instructed grimly, before hurrying out the back entrance himself.

But no matter how hard Rafe looked both ways up the street and in several shops, he couldn't find him, the other man having apparently disappeared. He knew where the man's car was, of course, and debated whether or not he should just go straight to the car park and hope to get there before the other man did.

But Rafe's first concern had to be Daisy and Cairo, so he returned to the restaurant.

'I lost him.' Rafe scowled as Cairo looked at him, her face having taken on a greyish tinge, her hands trembling as she held Daisy tightly against her. 'I'm pretty sure it isn't what you think, Cairo,' he added more reassuringly. 'I'll explain later.' He shot Cairo a warning look before going down on his haunches beside the little girl. 'Okay, Daisy-May?' he prompted gently.

'Can we have lunch now, Uncle Rafe?' she asked hopefully.

He gave an appreciative chuckle. 'Sure we can. Okay with you, Cairo?' He looked up at her.

Cairo felt too sick with reaction to answer him immediately.

She hadn't even realized there was anything wrong until Rafe had stood up and rushed into the restaurant and she had seen the man talking to Daisy.

A man who had seemed strangely familiar....

'Fine,' she answered distractedly, knowing from Rafe's warning expression that he didn't want either of them to alarm Daisy when she seemed to have taken the incident in her six-year-old stride.

Unlike Cairo.

It was every parent's nightmare!

They had only taken their eyes off Daisy for a minute or so. What if—

'It really isn't what you think,' Rafe assured her quietly, taking a light hold of her arm as they followed Daisy back to their table. 'At least, I'm pretty sure that it isn't,' he added grimly.

'You'll have to give me a better explanation than that, Rafe.' She gave an involuntary shudder. 'What if he had taken Daisy? I would never have forgiven myself if—'

'Don't even think about it.' Rafe squeezed her arm. 'I would never have let that happen.'

Cairo believed him.

After all that had happened between them, the way Rafe had proved so unfaithful as a lover, Cairo still believed him implicitly when he assured her that he would keep Daisy safe….

Rafe wished he could be as sure of being able

to keep his promise to Cairo as he sounded! But until he found out who the man in the blue car was, and why he had been following them most of the day, he really had no idea whom he was actually supposed to be protecting.

Daisy…or Cairo?

Daisy was the one to give him part of the answer. 'I think that man was one of your fans, Uncle Rafe,' she told him once she had eaten a piece of pizza.

'Why do you think that, Daisy?' he asked, at the same time aware that Cairo was picking at her salad rather than eating it, obviously still very shaken by what had happened. Even so, Rafe couldn't help but admire the fact that she was trying to appear as if everything were normal.

'He asked me if you were Rafe Montero,' Daisy explained happily before picking up another piece of her pizza.

Rafe shot Cairo a frowning glance before answering the little girl. 'And what did you say, Daisy-May?'

'I said you were.' She nodded. 'Because you are, aren't you?'

'Yes,' Rafe agreed with a smile. 'For my sins, that's exactly who I am.'

Daisy nodded. 'Then he asked me the name of my mummy.'

'Your…mummy?' Rafe repeated slowly with a quick glance at Cairo.

'Mmm.' Daisy gave a mischievous grin. 'I told him that her name was Margo. Because it is, isn't it?' she added with satisfaction.

'Daisy—'

'Don't you see, Uncle Rafe, that man thought Aunty Cairo was my mummy?' She giggled at the joke she had played on the other man.

Yes, Rafe did see—better than Daisy, in fact. As he knew that Cairo must.

'He was a reporter!' Cairo spoke for the first time since they had returned to the table, anger starting to replace her emotional turmoil as she realized Daisy hadn't been in danger, after all; she had simply been pumped for information about Cairo and Rafe.

'I had a suspicion that he might be, yes,' Rafe admitted grimly.

Cairo's eyes widened. 'You had a—? He was at the supermarket this morning!' she breathed incredulously as she suddenly remembered why the other man had seemed so familiar to her a few minutes ago. She also remembered Rafe's distraction earlier as he'd watched the reporter getting into his car!

Her mouth tightened. 'How long have you known he was following us?'

'Not now, Cairo!' he snapped, a nerve pulsing in his tightly clenched jaw.

'But—'

'I said not now,' he ordered harshly.

Cairo clamped her lips together as she continued to glare at him from behind her sunglasses.

Rafe had known that man was following them. He had known, dammit, and he hadn't so much as warned her....

'For God's sake, calm down,' Rafe told her impatiently an hour or so later as the two of them sat on the golden-white sand amongst the rocks in a relatively private cove, Daisy off building sandcastles nearer the water.

'Calm down!' Cairo repeated furiously as she turned to face him. 'You knew that man was following us. You knew, Rafe, and yet you said nothing!' She breathed agitatedly.

'Because I knew you would react like this,' he retorted. 'Look, don't worry about it, okay? I'll make a couple of calls when I get back to the villa, and—'

'Oh, you'll make a couple of calls,' Cairo repeated sarcastically. 'That's all right, then. The arrogant Rafe Montero will just "make a couple of calls" and everyone can once again sleep safely in their beds—'

'Not everyone, Cairo,' he cut in.

She scowled at him. 'I'm really not in the mood for your innuendos just now, Rafe.'

'Then what are you in the mood for?' he challenged softly.

Her eyes widened as she saw the intent in his. 'Don't even think about—' She broke off abruptly as Rafe reached out to remove her sunglasses and throw them down on the towel before his mouth came down fiercely on hers.

Cairo kissed him back just as fiercely.

Furiously.

All the emotions of the last couple of hours were in that kiss.

The absolute terror when she had seen that man talking to Daisy.

The relief when she'd reached Daisy's side and was able to hold the little girl to her protectively.

Followed by this burning, almost uncontrollable rage towards Rafe for not even telling her he had thought they were being followed.

How dared he?

How *dared* he!

She wrenched her mouth free of his to put her hands against his chest and push him away from her. 'I thought I told you there would be no repeat of—of this sort of thing!' she snapped fierily.

'What sort of thing would that be, Cairo?' he jeered.

Cairo drew in a ragged breath. 'I'm sure your lethal charm usually silences a woman, Rafe,' she scorned, her cheeks flushed, eyes fever-bright. 'But—'

'Is my charm really lethal, Cairo?' he interrupted.

'Not to me!' she denied, continuing to glare at him as she sat with her arms wrapped protectively about her knees.

His devilish smile said otherwise. 'All evidence to the contrary, my dear Cairo.'

'I'm not your "dear", anything,' she came back vehemently. 'And I don't care what promise you made Jeff yesterday.' She shook her head. 'Now that we know a reporter has tracked you down—'

'Or you.'

Her eyes narrowed. 'It was *you* the reporter recognized—'

'If that's what he is.' Rafe shrugged.

'Whatever,' Cairo snapped. 'He's following *you*, Rafe. Which means you're the one who will have to leave—'

'I've already told you I'm not going anywhere,' Rafe retorted firmly.

He hadn't meant to kiss Cairo again just now. Hadn't meant to. But he had been unable to stop himself. She had looked so damned beautiful as she'd glared at him so fiercely. So achingly desirable.

Cairo was right; he should leave. He should get himself as far away as possible from the temptation she still—incredibly!—represented.

But after the incident at the restaurant Rafe knew he had even more reason to stay. If the man who had been following them this morning did turn out to be a member of the paparazzi, then a little thing like Rafe chasing him off earlier wasn't going to shake him. The man knew exactly who Rafe was now, and, despite what Daisy might have told the man about her 'mummy', Rafe knew that if the other man was any good at his job, then it wouldn't be long before he found out who Cairo really was, too.

But he was sure Cairo must already know that….

His mouth twisted wryly. 'It's just one reporter, Cairo—'

'Who will no doubt quickly be followed by others!' she pointed out, her voice rising with her agitation. 'Daisy and I were doing just fine before you arrived.'

'Sure you were,' Rafe said sarcastically.

'And just what is that supposed to mean?'

Rafe's gaze ran over her with slow deliberation. 'Daisy is a great kid, but you—you're too thin, Cairo. You have dark circles under your eyes because you don't sleep properly. You're as nervy as hell.' He heaved a disgusted sigh. 'I wouldn't call that "doing just fine", would you?'

'I believe I've already told you before that when I want your opinion, I'll ask for it—'

'No, Cairo, you'll get it whether you want it or not,' he told her forcefully as he dropped down onto the sand beside her to take her chin in his grasp and turn her face towards his. 'What happened to the Cairo Vaughn I knew and loved?'

'*Loved*, Rafe?' She laughed incredulously. 'You don't even know the meaning of the word!' Her gaze was challenging.

Rafe continued to look at her wordlessly for several seconds before abruptly releasing her, knowing he wasn't going to reach her this way. If there was any of the old Cairo left to reach...

Cairo glared at him with frustrated anger. Rafe

hadn't loved her. If he had loved her, then she wouldn't have gone to his hotel suite that day eight years ago and found a naked woman in his bed!

'This beach is slightly different from the one we once walked on together at midnight, isn't it?' he said huskily now.

Cairo eyed him warily, not quite sure how to reply to that comment.

She knew exactly which beach Rafe was referring to, of course. Just as she clearly remembered what had happened at the end of that walk. She was just surprised that Rafe remembered it, too, after all this time....

'I seem to remember I ruined a pair of perfectly good shoes walking across the pebbles and rocks,' she said coolly.

'It was worth it,' Rafe murmured softly.

Yes, it had been, but—

'Have you ever been back there?' Rafe asked, quirking up one eyebrow to signal his interest.

'To the Isle of Man?'

She had only vaguely even heard of the Isle of Man, a small island located between England

and Ireland, before she had been there on location during the filming of *A Love For All Time*. The island's old-fashioned quaintness had been a perfect spot for the post-war love story, in which Rafe had had the role of male lead and Cairo had had the supporting actress role to Pamela Raines's female lead.

A situation that had, unfortunately, become echoed in real life!

'I try not to dwell on past mistakes,' she dismissed in a deliberately offhand tone of voice.

'It was damn cold on the beach that night, wasn't it?' he said, ignoring her supposed lack of interest in the topic.

Until they'd found the ideal way to keep warm, yes....

'Rafe—'

'Life seemed a lot simpler then, too,' he continued wistfully as if she hadn't spoken.

Her eyes widened. 'Simpler?'

He nodded. 'There was just you and me—'

'And Pamela,' Cairo put in dryly. 'Let's not forget the beautiful and rapacious Pamela, shall we?'

Rafe's mouth tightened. 'I forgot about her years ago.'

Cairo gave a derisive smile. 'How convenient to have such an—accommodating memory!'

His eyes narrowed and his voice turned positively icy. 'Pamela meant nothing to me.'

'Has *any* woman ever meant anything to you, Rafe?' Cairo enquired hotly.

How could he sit and claim Pamela had meant nothing to him?

The other woman had been naked in his hotel room that day, her hair all tousled, that look— that look of sleepy satisfaction on her face the result of Rafe's lovemaking that Cairo had seen so often on her own face when she'd looked in the mirror.

His gaze became hooded now. 'Just the one,' he murmured, his meaning obvious as he steadily held her gaze.

'Oh, please!' Cairo muttered in disgust as she stood up and moved away from him. 'I'm not that naïve twenty-year-old any more, Rafe. So don't even think about trying your seduction routine on me again—'

'It isn't a routine, dammit—'

'Of course it is!' She turned on him angrily. 'You sailed into Douglas Bay that day looking like a Spanish pirate captaining his ship and completely swept me and every other woman on the island off their feet!'

Cairo could remember it as if it were yesterday, standing at the window of her hotel room, watching as the three-masted sailing ship came round the headland and anchored in the bay, a small launch leaving the ship minutes later, the man at the wheel—looking every inch that Spanish pirate!—clearly the darkly handsome Rafe Montero.

Cairo had lost her heart to Rafe's dark and rugged wildness before she was even introduced to him an hour later.

And she wasn't going to fall for it again.

Ever.

'I'm going for a swim,' she told Rafe abruptly as she took off her T-shirt before peeling her skirt down over her hips and legs and revealing that she wore a brief white bikini beneath.

Rafe stood and watched Cairo as she ran down the golden sand to wade thigh-deep in the water before diving smoothly beneath its surface, his hands clenching at his sides as he appreciated how the white of her bikini emphasised the golden tan of her skin. Smooth, silky skin he could still feel against the palms of his hands.

Cairo was right; she was no longer a naïve twenty-year-old. Just as he was no longer twenty-nine and bowled off his feet by her beauty the moment he was introduced to her.

But a part of him wished that he were….

CHAPTER SIX

'I THINK you're being absolutely ridiculous, Rafe,' Cairo told him coolly as she hung their wet costumes and towels on the line strung between two trees at the back of the villa. Daisy was inside watching a cartoon channel on the television.

They had all showered and changed since returning an hour ago, Cairo now wearing a loose cream-coloured blouse over fitted jeans, the dampness of her long hair twisted into a knot and secured at her crown, her face completely bare of make-up.

She looked about eighteen, Rafe decided impatiently. Although that in no way stopped her being so damned stubborn he wanted to shake her until her teeth rattled!

His gaze narrowed on her warningly. 'If you won't agree to come down to Cannes with me this evening, then I'm not going, either,' he repeated evenly.

'Scrap my previous statement—your behaviour is positively juvenile!' Cairo glared at him. 'I won't if you won't,' she mocked as she reached for another of the towels and began to hang it on the line. 'You have to go to Cannes this evening, Rafe—I don't!'

'I don't have to go anywhere until I've managed to find out the identity of the man who spoke to Daisy at lunchtime,' Rafe assured her just as stubbornly.

Rafe had called several people he knew in the newspaper business, but as yet none of them had been offered a story about himself and Cairo. They would call him back when, or if, they did.

Admittedly his own temper was slightly frayed around the edges after those memories earlier of their time together on the Isle of Man. But Cairo's adamant refusal to even think about re-considering her decision not to go down to

Cannes with him tonight was only increasing Rafe's frustration, which was already exacerbated by a sexual tension that was becoming more unbearable by the minute.

She sighed. 'So much for your "couple of phone calls".'

'If he's a reporter, then we'll know by tomorrow morning, anyway,' Rafe pointed out. 'I only said *if* he's a reporter, Cairo,' he said as she gave a pained groan.

She shook her head. 'We both know that he is. Do you think he has photographs, too?'

'If he's any good at his job then, yes, of course he has photographs.' There was no point in even attempting to lie, Rafe knew, when tomorrow morning's newspapers would tell their own story, no doubt including wild speculation about their relationship.

He could see it now, photographs of himself and Cairo shopping for food, of them walking through Grasse with Daisy, of the three of them laughing together as they sat down at the table in the square outside the restaurant.

All very cosily domestic.

Deceptively so.

Anyone who had ever listened to a single conversation between himself and Cairo would know differently—they couldn't even discuss the weather without getting into an argument about it!

'I don't see anything in the least funny about this situation, Rafe!' Cairo snapped as she saw his rueful smile. 'The reason I'm annoyed is pretty obvious after the publicity following my divorce from Lionel.' She grimaced. 'But I'm sure there must be someone in your own life who isn't going to be amused, either, by photographs of the two of us together.'

Cairo hadn't spent long, boring hours in her trailer waiting to be called on set for months now—that was the only time she flicked through the glossy magazines that contained those sorts of gossipy articles—so she had no idea whether or not Rafe was involved with anyone at the moment. But he probably was....

His mouth twisted mockingly. 'I doubt any of my family will be concerned.'

Cairo sighed. 'I wasn't talking about your family and you know it.'

Rafe had occasionally talked about his family when they were together. Of his Spanish father who had visited America as a student and fallen in love with the blonde-haired, blue-eyed daughter of a Texas rancher, the two of them marrying once they finished college, and now working that ranch in Texas themselves, along with Rafe's younger brother, Pedro, and his wife and young family.

Rafe grinned. 'I'm well aware of that, Cairo,' he drawled. 'And, no, I very much doubt that photographs of you and I together are going to bother anyone but the two of us.'

'What a shame,' she came back insincerely.

Rafe sobered. 'Cairo, I would never have kissed you last night if I was involved with someone else.'

She raised sceptical brows. 'Really?'

'Dammit, Cairo—'

'Rafe, I have no intention of getting into yet another argument with you,' she told him wearily. 'Just accept that I am not going to Cannes with you tonight—'

'Why the hell not?'

'One, I don't want to go. Two, I didn't bring anything suitable to wear. Three,' she added simply, 'I'm still waiting for Jeff to return one of my calls.'

She had made two so far. One at the restaurant when she had reached his answering service, and hadn't bothered to leave a message as she had quickly rung off to be with Daisy. And another one at the beach when she had returned from her swim and had left a message asking Jeff to call her back as soon as possible to let her know how Margo was.

She had brought her mobile outside with her now in the hopes he would call back soon.

Rafe scowled. 'One, I don't give a damn what you want; I'm not going out and leaving you and Daisy here alone this evening. Two, you can go naked for all I care. And three, that's what mobile phones are for!' he all but snarled.

'There's no need to shout—and I told you not to touch me again, Rafe!' Cairo's eyes flashed a warning as she looked down at the fingers that had reached out to curl like steel bands about her arm.

Rafe breathed unevenly as he looked down at her for several long seconds. 'You would try the patience of a saint, Cairo!'

'You should be just fine, then, shouldn't you?' she baited him. 'I told you to let go of my arm, Rafe.' She looked up to meet his gaze unflinchingly.

The very air seemed to have stilled about them, not a sound to be heard except their own breathing as they continued that silent battle of wills, their faces only inches apart as blue eyes held brown.

Cairo felt as if the whole of her insides were melting as Rafe stood far too close to her, those fingers encircling her arm sending waves of awareness to her breasts and thighs.

Only Rafe had ever been able to make her feel like this with just a look. Only Rafe had ever been able to make her want him with just the touch of his hand against her flesh.

A hand he now let drop back to his side even as his gaze continued to hold hers captive. 'Do you know what I want to do to you right this minute?' he murmured.

Cairo moistened dry lips, unable to speak or look away from that mesmerizing gaze.

'If you won't let me touch you, then let me tell you all the things I've been imagining doing with you,' Rafe said gruffly. 'Wild, wonderful things—'

'Rafe—'

'Erotic beautiful things,' he continued mercilessly, his eyes gleaming with the desire he no longer held in check. 'You see that wall behind you...? Yes, that wall,' he confirmed softly as Cairo gave the low stone wall a quick glance. 'I want to slip off your jeans and panties before sitting you on top of that wall and kneeling in front of you. I want to slowly unbutton your blouse to bare your breasts to the sun so that I can touch them, kiss them, lick your nipples, suckle them into the heat of my mouth—'

'*Rafe*...!' Cairo's intended groan of protest instead came out as an aching entreaty for him to continue, her skin becoming sensitized just by his words, by the evocative image he was creating, her nipples hard against the soft material of her blouse, and a moist heat pooling between her thighs.

His eyes were dark. 'Then I want to kiss my way—slowly—down to your navel.' His voice was low, hypnotic. 'Dipping my tongue, tasting you, before I go lower, parting your legs even as I part your glossy curls and find the very centre of you with my lips and tongue. I still remember the taste of you there, Cairo. So sweet and hot…' He groaned.

'Rafe, you have to stop this now!' she choked, all of her feeling on fire now, aching with a need for the things he had described so eloquently.

'Why do I, Cairo?' His gaze still held hers. 'I'm only talking, telling you of the things I would like to do with you.'

Cairo could feel every single one of them! Could feel his hands and lips against her breasts, suckling her nipples, his mouth hot and liquid across the flatness of her stomach as he moved lower, tasting that pool of moisture there, licking her, sucking ever so gently on her arousal and taking her over the edge into wild oblivion. She could feel all of that just as strongly as she felt the sun beating down on them.

Just as she could imagine touching Rafe, her hands gliding lovingly over the broadness of his bare shoulders and torso, her lips following that same path, kissing him, caressing him as she slowly made her way down to the hard thrust of his arousal, lips and tongue tasting him as she took him in her mouth and felt his response to those caresses, hearing his groans of longing, his need for release…

Why had everything gone so wrong between them eight years ago? she wondered achingly. Why, when she had loved him so much, given so much—when they had been able to give each other such physical pleasure—hadn't she been enough for him?

They were questions Cairo had asked herself many times over the years. The answers were all too obvious.

With the prospect of a month's filming on the

Isle of Man—a beautiful unspoilt island but nevertheless one that offered very little in the way of entertainment for a man as rakish as Rafe Montero—Cairo must have been an easy conquest, a diversion in what might otherwise have been a tedious time for him when he wasn't actually filming.

Admittedly the relationship had continued for a while longer once they'd all returned to London to complete the filming, Cairo more often than not spending the night in Rafe's penthouse suite at his hotel with him, the two of them even occasionally going out to dinner with Margo and Jeff.

But somewhere along the way Cairo had missed the signs that Rafe was tired of the relationship. She knew why she had missed them, of course; her own love for Rafe had made her completely blind to anyone and everything else!

She had certainly been blind to the fact that Rafe's attention had moved on to someone else, that it was now his co-star, Pamela Raines, who interested him, and whom he wanted to share his bed. As it had turned out, Rafe had been so determined the actress would share his bed that he hadn't even had the time to tell Cairo to vacate it before moving Pamela Raines into it…

Cairo certainly couldn't allow herself to be seduced into becoming Rafe's South of France 'diversion', too!

What thoughts were going through her head, Rafe wondered as he looked at her searchingly. Whatever they were, they were making her frown.

'Were you and Bond happy together?' he suddenly rasped harshly.

Her eyes widened. 'I don't think—'

'It isn't going to hurt you to tell me that much, surely, Cairo?' Rafe pressed, knowing the moment of intimacy was over. For now…

She shook her head. 'Haven't you been reading the newspapers the last ten months, Rafe?'

He shrugged. 'In my experience they rarely report the truth.'

She gave a laugh of pure cynicism. 'That's been my experience, too!'

'Well?'

'I haven't asked you about any of your relationships the last eight years, so why on earth should I answer any of your questions about my marriage to Lionel?' she retorted indignantly.

'Ask away,' Rafe invited.

'I—' Cairo broke off as her mobile began to ring. 'That could be Jeff,' she pointed out huskily.

'Then you had better answer it, hadn't you?' he bit out curtly, before turning away to thrust his hands in his pockets.

Dammit, every time he and Cairo came even close to understanding each other, something, or someone, interrupted them!

Why the hell he wanted answers to these questions after all this time was beyond him. Maybe it was because of those memories this afternoon of when they'd met on the Isle of Man, when the connection between them had seemed so instant and exclusive….

As it had seemed to be just now, too….

Or maybe it was because the abrupt end of his relationship with Cairo three months later had always seemed like unfinished business to him….

One day they had seemed to be totally together and the next she had told him it was all over, using empty phrases like 'we both need our own space' and 'it was fun while it lasted but now it's over' as she'd walked out of his life.

Phrases that had only made sense to Rafe when that very same evening Cairo had gone out to dinner with the producer of the film, and only weeks later she had married him!

To add insult to injury, the 'happy couple' had even invited him, and the rest of the crew from *A Love For All Time* to the wedding! Rafe had excused himself from that invitation and spent the afternoon in bed with his co-star Pamela Raines instead.

But being here with Cairo like this, talking to her, touching her again, imagining making love with her, seemed to have released all those old memories, the good, as well as the bad.

Half of him had wanted to punish her just now as he told her of how he would make love to her, the other half punishing himself for still wanting her. He was still hard from those imaginings, his arousal a low throb that he had no control over—

'Margo's had the baby,' Cairo spoke huskily behind him. 'A little boy,' she added as Rafe turned in sharp enquiry. 'Margo is fine,' she continued emotionally. 'The baby—Simon Raphael—is in an incubator, but Jeff seems very hopeful that he's going to be okay, too—' She broke off to bury her face in her hands as she began to cry.

'But that's good, isn't it?' Rafe frowned, this time having no choice but to take her in his arms.

Cairo had no idea why she was crying. Relief, probably. She had been so worried about Margo and the baby.

But it wasn't just that, she knew. The strain of being here with Rafe, talking to him, having him describe what it would be like making love to her, feeling every caress and touch of his lips on her body, was also taking its toll. Finding herself in his arms certainly wasn't helping her dispel the effect!

She straightened, avoiding his searching gaze

as she wiped the tears from her cheeks to step away from him. 'It's much better news than I'd hoped for,' she agreed.

His eyes narrowed. 'Does Jeff want you and Daisy to go back to England now?'

'Not for a few more days, until he's absolutely sure…' Cairo shook her head. 'I have to go in and tell Daisy the good news,' she said as she turned away.

'Cairo?'

She closed her lids briefly before turning back to look at him with guarded eyes. 'Yes?'

Rafe's gaze was mocking. 'Now there are only two reasons why you can't come to Cannes with me this evening….'

She drew in a sharp breath. 'Rafe, you have no idea of the avalanche of publicity we would be bringing down on ourselves by appearing in public together!'

Rafe gave a rueful smile. 'I think I have a pretty good idea. Besides, with the appearance of tomorrow's newspapers, the chances are we're going to be presented with a fait accompli, anyway.' His mouth tightened grimly. 'Personally I would rather spike the bast—the guy's guns, by appearing in public with you tonight and so ruining his chances of an exclusive tomorrow.'

He had a point, Cairo realized unwillingly.

She was weakening in her resolve not to accompany him, Rafe noted with satisfaction as she hesitated. And he was determined that she would, meant it when he told Cairo she couldn't go on hiding like this. Yeah, her divorce had been messy and very public, but she needed to get some perspective back in her life.

With their past history, why the hell should he care what Cairo did, either now or in the future?

He shouldn't.

And yet he knew that he did....

He should never have given into the temptation of telling her all the things he would like to do to her.

'Well?' he prompted tersely.

Cairo sighed heavily, knowing that he wasn't going to give up.

'Okay, I—I'll ask Daisy what she wants to do—'

'Coward,' Rafe told her softly.

Her chin came up, her eyes flashing darkly. 'You know nothing about me, Rafe. Nothing!' she snapped angrily.

He shrugged. 'Then prove me wrong, Cairo, and come with me tonight.'

Her mouth twisted into a derisive smile. 'I guarantee you'll regret your insistence more than I will.'

He raised an eyebrow. 'I'm willing to take that chance if you are.'

Was she? She could see the logic of what Rafe was saying concerning spiking the guns of the reporter who had followed them today. The two of them appearing together in public this evening would certainly diffuse the exclusivity of any story he might have written. Except the very idea of appearing in public with Rafe as her partner for the evening, so totally aware of him as she now was, was Cairo's idea of a nightmare!

'I'll ask Daisy,' she repeated firmly. 'If *she* wants to go, then we will.'

Rafe could tell by the finality in her tone that it was the best answer he was going to get for now.

'Okay.' He sighed. 'Go and talk to Daisy now so that I know whether or not I have to call and make my excuses for this evening, after all.'

Rafe made no effort to follow Cairo into the villa, instead moving to sit on one of the chairs on the terrace, needing these few minutes' respite to bring his throbbing need for her under control.

Impossible when he could practically taste her….

CHAPTER SEVEN

'You have to believe me, Cairo, when I tell you I had no idea Bond had been invited this evening!'

Cairo knew by the grimness of Rafe's expression as he looked down at her so intently that he was telling the truth.

Not that she had ever thought otherwise; the two of them might have had their differences in the past, Rafe uncaring of her feelings for him, but she had never found him to be a vindictive man.

Believing what he did, to have deliberately brought her to this party in Cannes knowing Lionel was going to be here, too, would definitely have been vindictive on Rafe's part!

Until now it had been a surprisingly pleasant evening. Cairo had met up and chatted with several old acquaintances as she sipped the freely flowing champagne, and Daisy was absolutely enthralled with the whole thing as she pointed out people she recognized from films and television.

There had been the usual barrage of photographers outside, of course, an experience Cairo had also found less of an ordeal than she had expected. Rafe had kept a firm hold of her arm and smilingly fended off most of the more personal questions while at the same time keeping an eye out for the man who had followed them earlier today. He wasn't there, Rafe had informed her as they went into the huge white marquee on Cannes beach where the party was being held.

No doubt the man believed he had enough of an exclusive for one day!

Which he probably did....

Cairo had decided to put him firmly from her mind—along with that earlier, erotic, conversation with Rafe!—once she realized she was actually enjoying herself, having reacquainted herself with several friends that she hadn't seen since her move to London.

Until she chanced to glance across at the entrance of the marquee and see Lionel making a belated appearance!

'Maybe he wasn't invited.' She sighed, knowing that Lionel was quite capable of inviting himself if he had learnt that Cairo was here, seeing as she had so far evaded all of his previous efforts to see or speak to her.

'Do you want to leave?' Rafe asked.

Did she?

Admittedly, seeing Lionel again like this so unexpectedly had been a shock, but if she left now, it would look as if she was running away from an awkward situation. Worse, she would feel as if she was running away!

'No, I don't want to leave,' she answered Rafe firmly. 'Let's just continue to circulate, hmm?' she suggested tautly as she slid her hand into the crook of his arm.

'Fine with me.' Rafe nodded as he looked down at her with approval.

Despite her claim that she had nothing suitable to wear, Cairo looked stunningly beautiful this evening, the simple black sheath of a dress she wore giving her a classically elegant appearance when compared to all the glittering gowns being worn by the other women present. Her red hair was loose and silky about her shoulders, her eyes dark and luminous in her lightly tanned face, her lips glossed a challenging red.

Warpaint she might need before this evening was over, Rafe acknowledged heavily as he saw Lionel Bond making his way determinedly towards them.

Her ex-husband came to a halt in front of Cairo, his smile smooth and self-assured. 'I had no idea you were going to be here this evening, Cairo,' he greeted lightly. 'I seem to recall your telling me you hated this sort of thing?' he added quizzically.

Cairo returned that smile even as her grip tightened on Rafe's arm and her nails dug into the sleeve of his dinner jacket. 'I've made tonight an exception,' she replied coolly.

Rafe's gaze narrowed as he saw the way Bond was looking at Cairo with such warmth. Not entirely surprisingly, he found his own feelings towards her ex were far from friendly.

He could see why she'd been attracted to the man, of course. For not only was Lionel Bond incredibly rich and powerful, he was also six feet tall, still athletically fit in his late forties, with a boyishly handsome face and blond hair tinged a distinguishing grey at the temples.

Yes, Rafe could see the reason Cairo had once been attracted to this man. That she might still be attracted to him, in spite of their recent divorce…?

Cairo was sure that her knees were shaking so much they were actually knocking together! It hadn't even occurred to her that Lionel might be here this evening. She definitely wouldn't have come if it had.

And yet…

This first meeting since their divorce, a meeting she had steadfastly avoided in spite of Lionel's repeated efforts for it to be otherwise, had to have happened at some time, so why not get it over and done with?

The guilt she had carried with her for so long where Lionel was concerned, unable to love him and yet unable to leave him, either, because of that guilt, along with the fear that she might be the reason for his gambling addiction, no longer seemed like quite such a heavy weight as she looked at him now. Lionel looked surprisingly fit and well, and was obviously surviving quite well without her.

Perhaps he really had finally been able to stop the addiction that had for so long threatened to ruin him….

'I wonder why you've made tonight an exception?' Lionel turned to look at Rafe, his pale grey gaze wide with speculation.

Cairo turned to include Rafe in their conversation. 'You know Rafe of course…?'

'Of course.' Lionel nodded briefly in the younger man's direction, neither one making any attempt to shake hands.

Cairo couldn't help but appreciate the differences she could see in the two men as they stood so close together, Rafe so dark and compellingly attractive, Lionel a golden blond and all that was suave and handsomely self-assured.

But the expression of dislike on both men's

faces was identical as hard blue eyes clashed with steely grey!

'I must say that I would have expected you to be a little more—original, shall we say—in your choice of lover, Cairo,' Lionel challenged as he looked at Rafe. 'I had rather hoped I'd taught you to be a little more discerning in your tastes over the years.'

Cairo's breath caught in her throat at the deliberate insult, and she could feel Rafe's tension in his arm beneath her hand as he also recognized the directness of Lionel's attack.

Lionel had never been happy about her previous involvement with Rafe eight years ago, had considered Rafe one of the 'wild' set that had dominated Hollywood at the time. But Rafe had matured into a formidable and dangerous opponent in the intervening years, and he looked every bit as suave as Lionel this evening in the tailored black evening suit, snowy white shirt and red bow tie.

She gave her ex-husband a confident smile. 'There has never been anything wrong with my taste.'

'Really?' The intensity of Lionel's gaze seemed to look for some inclusion of himself in that statement.

'Yes—really,' Cairo echoed softly. 'Now if you'll excuse us—'

'You're looking rather beautiful this evening, Cairo,' Lionel told her warmly.

'I— Thank you.' She gave him a censorious frown.

'I'm sure Montero agrees with me, don't you, Montero?' he added with a mocking glance.

Rafe had never felt so much like hitting another man as he did at that moment. Not that he was going to. For one thing, it would achieve nothing except to relieve his own anger towards this man for even looking at Cairo so warmly. For another, he wouldn't give Bond the satisfaction of knowing how much it bothered him.

Rafe also doubted that Cairo would appreciate it if he laid her ex-husband out cold at her feet!

He released his arm from Cairo's hand to curve it about her waist, effectively pulling her to his side. 'In my experience, Cairo looks beautiful whatever the—occasion,' he drawled provocatively.

This conversation was spiralling out of control, Cairo decided impatiently. Ridiculously so, seeing as she and Lionel were already divorced, and she didn't have any relationship at all with Rafe!

'Enjoyable as this conversation is—' her tone implied the opposite '—I think I would like to go outside for some air, Rafe.' She looked at him compellingly.

Rafe gave a terse inclination of his head. 'Of course—'

'Uncle Lionel?'

Cairo had completely forgotten—not surprisingly!—Daisy's presence until that moment, her young niece rejoining them now that she had finished speaking to the young actor they had introduced her to after she had asked to meet him so she could tell the other girls about it when she returned to school next week!

'Daisy?' Lionel raised surprised brows as he turned to look at his former niece.

Daisy grinned up at him unabashedly, looking

absolutely adorable in a lemon sundress and white sandals. 'Aunty Cairo didn't say you were going to be here, too!'

'No, I don't suppose she did,' Lionel said with a rueful glance in Cairo's direction. 'I had no idea this was a family gathering. Can I expect to see Margo and Jeff this evening, too?'

Cairo gave him a quelling glance, Margo and Jeff never having made any secret of the fact that they didn't particularly like or approve of Lionel. 'No, there's just the three of us,' she answered pointedly.

'Hmm,' he murmured enigmatically. 'It's really is good to see you again, Cairo,' he added huskily. 'The two of us need to talk—'

'I don't think so, Lionel,' she cut in firmly; she and Lionel had absolutely nothing left to say to each other. They had spent months, years, trying to sort out the problems between them, all to no avail.

He reached out and grasped her arm. 'Tell me where you're staying, Cairo, and I'll—'

'Take your hand off her, Bond!' Rafe snarled between clenched teeth.

Lionel shot him a look of pure dislike. 'Butt out, Montero—'

'I'll give you until the count of three—'

'And then what?' Lionel challenged. 'This is absolutely none of your business—'

'I'm making it my business,' Rafe said in a lethal tone.

'Please don't, Rafe.' Cairo put her hand on his arm, her look one of pleading before she turned back to her ex-husband. 'We both know we have nothing left to say to each other, Lionel, and I certainly don't appreciate the way you're drawing attention to all of us,' she added as she became aware of the many curious gazes turned in their direction. 'I believe it's time that we left, Rafe.'

'I'll call you,' Lionel called after her.

Rafe turned to give the other man an icy glare, his hands clenching at his sides as he saw the almost desperate look on Bond's handsome face as he gazed after Cairo.

'Do we really have to go?' Daisy frowned her disappointment. 'I'm not in the least tired,' she assured them, widening her eyes as if to prove the point, and looking absolutely adorable as she did so.

Rafe chuckled softly as he released his hold on Cairo's waist to swing Daisy up into his arms. 'Aunty Cairo needs her beauty sleep,' he told her teasingly.

Daisy turned to look at her aunt. 'Aunty Cairo can't be any more beautiful than she already is,' she informed him proudly.

No, she couldn't, Rafe acknowledged heavily. She was absolutely gorgeous. Assured. Desirable.

'Then maybe it's me who needs my beauty sleep,' he said ruefully.

'You're much better looking than Uncle Lionel,' Daisy confided with innocent candour.

Rafe looked at Cairo over Daisy's head, wondering how she was taking the comparison, but unable to read anything from her composed expression as she coolly met his gaze.

'I like you better than Uncle Lionel, too,' Daisy continued with that same innocence. 'He never played with me like you do.'

Cairo thought this conversation had gone far

enough. Even if she did completely agree with everything Daisy had just said!

Rafe's rugged handsomeness was much more appealing than Lionel's suave urbanity. And, despite their differences, like Daisy, Cairo liked Rafe much better than she did Lionel, too….

'All the flattery in the world isn't going to stop us from leaving, young lady,' she teased her niece, although it was still several minutes before they got outside as people engaged them in conversation as they made their way towards the exit.

Daisy was fast asleep in the back of the car within minutes of their leaving the bright lights of Cannes. 'So much for her not being tired,' Cairo murmured wryly as she turned from making the little girl more comfortable within the confines of her seat belt. 'Phew.' She sighed deeply. 'I can't say I'm sorry that's over!' She leant back wearily against the headrest and closed her eyes.

Rafe gave her a brief glance, a frown creasing his brow when he turned back to the road as he was once again struck by Cairo's air of fragility.

'Is that the first time you and Bond have met since the divorce?' he asked.

'Yes.'

'I'm sorry it had to be in such a public way.' Rafe grimaced.

'I'm not.' Cairo turned her head to look at him. 'Thank you for being so—supportive,' she told him huskily.

Rafe's mouth tightened as he once again wondered how she really felt about seeing Bond again….

He shrugged. 'Bond didn't really give me any choice in the matter.'

'No,' Cairo accepted ruefully. 'But I thank you, anyway.'

Rafe couldn't think of a single thing to say in answer to that comment as they made the rest of the drive back to the villa in silence.

A tense, almost expectant silence, as even the air between them seemed to crackle with a taut, nerve-tingling tension that was electric in its intensity.

'I'll carry her inside,' Rafe offered as he parked

the car in the driveway of the villa to get out and lift Daisy from the back seat.

'Thank you,' Cairo murmured, barely able to look at the broadness of Rafe's back as she followed him through the villa to Daisy's bedroom.

What had happened between them in the car just now?

Because something had. Something so tangible Cairo felt she could almost reach out and touch it. Could reach out and touch Rafe.

As she knew he wanted to touch her….

'I'll be waiting outside on the terrace when you've finished putting Daisy to bed,' he breathed softly as he straightened after laying Daisy down on the cool sheets.

Cairo looked at him wordlessly, her gaze searching the hard, unreadable arrogance of his face. 'Rafe—' She broke off, her eyes wide, as Rafe moved to stand so close to her their bodies almost touched, that crackling tension she had been so aware of in the car intensifying as their gazes met and held.

Cairo could barely breathe. Rafe made no

effort now to hide the desire burning in the luminous depths of those deep blue eyes, the same desire that had been there earlier this afternoon when he'd told her of all the things he would like to do to her.

He lifted his hand, his palm cupping her chin as the pad of his thumb moved gently across her bottom lip. Cairo instinctively parted her lips at the softness of that caress even as she felt her nipples harden and swell beneath her dress.

Time seemed to stand still.

Not a sound, not a movement of air disturbed them.

All there was at that moment was Rafe and this wild, singing awareness that heated the blood in Cairo's veins and made her skin burn with the need for the caress of his hands upon it, stroking, cupping, arousing.

She didn't move—couldn't move as Rafe began to lower his head towards hers, her breath catching in her throat as his lips moved softly, enticingly, against hers. He was no longer touching her in any other way but held her captive there with just those arousing lips as he slowly sipped and tasted her.

How long that kiss lasted Cairo had no idea. Nor did she care as she responded with everything that was in her.

Cairo tasted wonderful, Rafe acknowledged achingly. Warm. Silky. Intoxicating.

He felt the hardening of his thighs even as he became drunk on the heady pleasure of kissing her. Nothing else. Just the softness of her lips against his as they drank their fill of each other.

Eventually it wasn't enough, of course. Rafe wanted more. So much more.

Rafe lifted his head to look down at Cairo, knowing from her flushed cheeks and the glow in the deep, dark brown of her eyes that she was as aroused as he was. 'I want you so much, Cairo,' he groaned throatily. 'Don't keep me waiting outside too long, hmm?'

Don't keep him—!

Rafe thought that the two of them—? That they were going to—?

Rafe believed her response to his kiss was an

invitation for the two of them to go outside together and make love in the way he had described earlier? Then what? A few more days of the same, before he returned to his world and she returned to hers?

Reality washed over Cairo like the shock of a blast of cold air, and she could only stare up at him as something withered and died deep down inside her. Some hope… Some remembered dream of long ago…

But this was Rafe Montero, she reminded herself. The same man who had claimed her heart eight years ago and then cast it aside when he became bored and moved on to another conquest. As he would become bored with her again once he had made love with her!

Not again, Cairo told herself firmly. Never again would she allow her heart to rule her head.

'I'll be outside,' Rafe whispered, running a slow, caressing finger down the hollow of her cheek before turning and quietly leaving the room.

Cairo stood as still as a statue.

She felt like one, too, at that moment.

A figure of cold marble in which no emotion, no sensation existed.

Not even pain....

CHAPTER EIGHT

'WHAT the hell do you think you're *doing*?'

Cairo was sitting up in bed reading a book—or, at least, appearing to!—when Rafe burst unannounced into her bedroom. A quick glance at the face of the slender gold watch on her wrist showed her that it was now half an hour since he had told her he would be waiting outside for her on the terrace.

She had considered actually lying down in bed with the light off and pretending she was asleep when he came in search of her—as she had known that he would—but had decided that would be too undignified; Rafe wasn't the type of man to just turn and leave again and was more than capable of switching on the light before dragging her from the bed kicking and screaming!

So instead she had removed her make-up and taken a leisurely shower before donning a pale cream nightgown of the sheerest silk, only a band of matching cream lace across her breasts preventing it from being completely transparent. She'd then stood in front of the mirror brushing her hair until it shone straight and sleek over her shoulders and down her spine.

Her tools of war, she decided angrily as she arranged her pillows before getting into bed to sit and wait, her tension increasing with each tick of her wristwatch.

However, none of that tension showed as she looked over her book at Rafe where he stood in the doorway glowering across the room at her. He was no longer wearing the jacket to his suit or the red bowtie, and the top two buttons of his shirt were open to reveal the silky black hair on his chest.

Cairo suppressed an inward shiver as she acknowledged how dark and dangerous he looked. Instead, she gave him a bright, enquiring smile. 'I'm reading a book, of course.'

Rafe's scowl deepened as he advanced into the

room, his movements predatory before he came to an abrupt halt beside the bed. 'I've been waiting outside for you for the last half-hour,' he growled.

Cairo could almost feel his anger, knew by the nerve that pulsed in his clenched jaw just how near to the surface that anger was.

She gave a shrug as she lay the book face down beside her on the bed. 'I decided I was just too tired for any more conversation tonight, Rafe.'

'You—!' Rafe bit off what he was going to say and instead drew in a deep, controlling breath. Like his father before him, Rafe had a volatile Spanish temper. A temper that Rafe rarely, if ever, lost. Only Cairo, it seemed, had the power to stretch his control to its very limits.

He very carefully reached down and plucked the book from beside her and placed it on the bedside table before sitting down on the edge of the bed. 'We both know conversation was the last thing I had in mind when I asked you to join me outside once Daisy was in bed,' he said softly.

'Really?' She continued to meet his gaze un-blinkingly.

'Yes,' he acknowledged pleasantly. 'Good book?' He nodded towards the bedside table.

'Very good,' she confirmed slowly, no longer quite as composed as Rafe saw a slight frown appear between the clear brown of her eyes.

'What's it about?' Rafe reached out and picked the book up so that he could read the back cover. 'Strange,' he said as he put it back down. 'I would never have tagged you as a reader of murder mysteries.'

She smiled. 'This one's about a woman who kills her lover after she finds out he's been cheating on her.'

'Really,' Rafe commented, easily holding her gaze with his. 'But I bet she gets caught in the end. They all do.'

'Not all of them,' Cairo said dryly. 'If you wouldn't mind, Rafe…? I really am very tired.' She raised one auburn brow.

Rafe wanted to reach out, grasp her shoulders, and shake her. Anything to put some spark of emotion back into her!

He had become more irritated by the minute as

he'd stood outside waiting for her to join him, knowing that earlier Cairo had wanted him as much as he wanted her.

But as he looked at her now he saw none of that softly desirable woman he had kissed such a short time ago. Instead he saw a woman whose barriers were so firmly back in place it was impossible to tell what thoughts were going through her head.

He gave her a narrow-eyed look. 'Did seeing Bond again tonight reawaken a spark of emotion for him? Is that it?'

She blinked in surprise. 'You're being utterly ridiculous, Rafe.' She gave him a pointed look. 'Now, if you wouldn't mind leaving? I really am very tired—'

'Cairo.' Rafe spoke her name quietly, but it was enough to silence her.

Cairo's gaze became less certain on his as she became aware of how dangerous it was for them to be alone together in her bedroom.

Very dangerous.

Not that she thought for one minute that Rafe

would use force to get what he wanted. Why should he when he knew he only had to touch her to ignite a passionate response from her?

Perhaps she should have turned the light off and pretended she was asleep, after all!

'Lionel and I are divorced, Rafe,' she reminded him.

'That doesn't mean you can't still be in love with him!'

She sighed. 'You obviously know nothing about me if you believe that. But, then, you never did know anything about me, did you?'

'I thought I did,' he muttered.

Her eyes flashed. 'And you thought wrong, didn't you?'

Yes, he had been wrong about Cairo eight years ago, Rafe acknowledged grimly. So very wrong.

Then.

And now…

He stood up abruptly. 'You're right, Cairo, this was a bad idea. I'll leave you to get back to your book.'

'Thank you,' she snapped.

Rafe paused to look back at her as he stood in the bedroom doorway, his smile self-derisive. 'I should probably be thanking you for preventing me from making yet another mistake where you're concerned.' And yet the ache of his body told him that gratitude was the last thing he really felt….

Cairo's eyes glittered darkly. 'I'll take it as said!'

'Goodnight, Cairo.'

'Goodnight, Rafe.'

Rafe gave her one last lingering glance before leaving the bedroom and the villa, stepping outside to take deep breaths of the perfumed night air, his gaze drawn to the swimming pool as the moonlight shimmered invitingly on the water.

He didn't even hesitate, throwing off his clothes as he reached the lower terrace before diving smoothly into the coolly refreshing water.

She was crying, Cairo realized numbly. Tears that burnt her skin as they tracked down the paleness of her cheeks.

She wiped those tears away impatiently as she got out of bed, too restless to even think about sleep now as she began to pace the confines of her bedroom.

She had to get out of here!

She needed air.

Space in which to breathe.

The villa was in darkness, not a sound to be heard as she trailed through the comfortable sitting-room and out onto the terrace, the silence there broken by a sound she had come to associate with this area of France: hundreds of frogs croaking in the moonlight.

Somehow that familiar sound comforted her, calmed her, a smile curving her lips as she walked down the steps to the lower terrace to where the sound of the frogs became even louder.

Rafe floated in the shallow end of the pool, watching Cairo as she approached. She looked almost ghostly in the moonlight, her feet bare, her cream nightgown transparent against the nakedness of her body, her face a pale oval. The eerie light gave her long hair the appearance of cinnamon touched with silver.

That she was unaware of his presence in the

water was in no doubt, a smile curving her lips as she held out her arms and turned her face up to the moonlight, long lashes shadowing her cheeks as she closed her lids.

She was Aphrodite.

Goddess of love.

Rafe's breath caught in his throat as he looked at her, her breasts full and pert against the sheer material of her nightgown, her waist narrow, hips gently curving, a shadowed triangle visible between her thighs.

His body hardened in response to that beauty, his earlier resolve crumbling into dust as he knew that, despite everything, he still wanted to make love with her.

Cairo raised her lids as she heard another sound besides the croaking of the frogs, turning slowly to the source of that sound, her eyes widening as she watched Rafe stepping slowly up from the pool.

A completely naked Rafe, water dripping down his body, his thrusting arousal obvious as he walked slowly towards her. His gaze held hers as he took her in his arms, his body wet and cold from the water. Then his head lowered and his mouth claimed hers.

They kissed hungrily, deeply, lips and tongues seeking, drinking, devouring, as Cairo's fingers became entwined in the silky darkness of Rafe's hair, their legs entwined, bodies pressed closely together.

Cairo groaned as she felt Rafe slip the thin straps of her nightgown down her arms. She felt his cool hand against her heated flesh, her back arching in invitation when, as he had described this afternoon, he cupped one of her breasts to run the soft pad of his thumb caressingly across that sensitized tip, engulfing her in a warmth that reached from her toes to her fingertips.

Rafe kissed her lingeringly on the lips, tasting her, his hand still caressing her as he raised his head to look down at her. Her eyes were half closed, her breathing soft and shallow, a slight flush to the hollows of her cheeks.

His gaze darkened as he lowered it to where his hand cupped and held her, the small, perfect roundness of her bared breasts tipped with nipples of deep coral, full and tight as they pouted towards him in tempting invitation.

Rafe lowered his head to run his tongue moistly around that roused nipple, closing his lips about its coral-pink tip and suckling deeply as he heard her moan. His tongue lapped and rasped over it as his long, slim fingers continued to caress the arousal of that other deep rose tip.

Then Rafe's hands spanned the slenderness of her waist and he lifted her up into him so that he could feast on those breasts, licking, sucking, feeling the spasms that rocked her body as he gently nibbled her roused flesh before once again suckling her deeply inside the warmth of his mouth.

He moved one of his hands from her waist to slide the silk nightgown up the smoothness of her legs and thighs as he sought and found the centre of her arousal.

She was already moist, her thighs parting as she allowed him to touch her there, to stroke and caress her before his questing hand moved lower and he gently probed that moistness with one finger, and then two, entering her, claiming her as he felt her rush of dampness against the rapidly increasing thrusts.

He gave the hard pebble of her nipple one last lingering kiss before moving lower, kneeling at her feet as his lips and tongue moved over the creamy silk of her waist and stomach, lightly probing her navel before he moved lower still. Cairo's hips arched in a silent plea as his tongue moved unerringly against the hard nub nestled amongst the silky dampness of her red-golden curls and he felt her response, tasting her, sucking that nub into his mouth until she gasped.

Cairo was lost.

She had been lost from the moment Rafe's mouth had touched hers and his hands had caressed her, his clever tongue and lips now driving her heatedly, relentlessly, towards a climax that claimed her so quickly, so fiercely, she could only cling mindlessly to his shoulders as the pleasure began deep inside her, her breath now coming in weak, gasping sobs. That pleasure swelled and grew, consuming her, flinging her into a maelstrom of feelings, sensations that seemed never ending as Rafe continued to suckle her and his tongue lapped against her in greedy hunger.

Her fingers clenched in the thickness of his hair, holding him to her as he drained every last vestige of pleasure from her totally acquiescent body.

And still she wanted more, ached for more, wanted to know that pleasure again as much as she needed Rafe buried deep inside her, groaning her disappointment as he stood up and she felt him moving away from her.

He couldn't leave her now!

She reached out and touched him, watching Rafe's eyes close as her fingers curled around him. He was steel encased in velvet and she ran her fingers down the long length of him, her other hand cupping and holding him as she caressed rhythmically, hearing Rafe's groan as her lips trailed moistly across his chest on a downward path to the centre of his arousal.

Rafe's knees almost buckled as Cairo knelt

before him and he felt her lips close about him before she oh-so-slowly drew him deep into the heated moisture of her mouth, his hands tightly gripping her shoulders before he held her away from him as he felt himself losing control.

'Not yet, Cairo,' he murmured throatily even as he lifted her up and away from him.

Not because he didn't like her mouth on him, or that velvety caressing tongue lapping and tasting the hard length of him. Truth be told, he liked it too much, was in danger of just letting go and spilling himself like some inexperienced boy. And he hadn't drunk his fill of Cairo yet. Hadn't touched her, kissed her, caressed her nearly enough to assuage eight years of hungry need.

She stood perfectly still as he lowered the nightgown completely to let it fall down about her feet, her breasts small and firm as he lowered his head and kissed each of them slowly in turn before holding her away from him to feast his eyes on her nakedness. She was the most beautiful woman he had ever known. So tiny and yet so totally, femininely perfect, her skin soft and silky, and the colour of magnolia, with those rosy tipped breasts so pert and thrusting it made him feel hungry for her just looking at them.

Rafe swung her up into his arms and sat down on the lounger, her legs straddling him, the warmth between her thighs reaching out to tempt him as his hard arousal moved restlessly against that heat.

'Take me into you, Cairo…' Rafe groaned. 'Deep, deep inside you!'

'Soon,' Cairo promised as she rubbed herself against him, wetting him, giving herself pleasure, as well as him, as her own arousal mated with his, her aching nipples a caress against the soft hair on Rafe's chest as she raced towards another climax.

Rafe's hand moved between them and she cried out as he found her hardened nub, thumb caressing even as his fingers slid smoothly inside her, those thrusts becoming harder, faster, Cairo almost sobbing as her climax peaked again and again.

'Now, Rafe,' she moaned. 'I want you inside me now!' she begged as she raised herself slightly to curl her hand about him and rub the tip of his hard shaft against her wetness, hearing

Rafe's groans as she teased them both until they could wait no longer. She opened herself to him and took him inside her slowly, her gaze holding his as he entered her inch by pleasurable inch.

Rafe felt as if he were almost going insane as Cairo slowly wrapped herself about his engorged arousal. He felt the quivers of her recent pleasure, longed to thrust deep inside her, hard and fast, needing to assuage his own burning need for release, but at the same time wanting this moment to last for ever.

He groaned again, his eyes closing, as Cairo slowly began to ride him, her knees placed on the lounger beside him to give her purchase as she raised almost to his tip before plunging down again. Again. And again. Riding him steadily faster. Harder. Her hips thrusting, drowning him in sensation, until he felt the first surge of his own release, his hands moving instinctively to her hips as he began to pump deep inside her, grasping her, holding her as he thrust into her in ever-increasing wildness, falling weakly backwards as she continued to milk every last drop from his body.

The fog of desire faded as the cool night air stroked the aroused heat of Cairo's body, and she groaned low in her throat as she realized exactly what she and Rafe had just done.

This wasn't real, she recognized achingly as she stared down at him in the moonlight. This madness with Rafe, the two of them being intimate like this, it wasn't real. It never had been.

Not eight years ago.

And not now, either.

'Cairo…?' Rafe questioned huskily as he obviously felt her withdrawal.

This wasn't real, she told herself again as she began to tremble in reaction.

She shook her head. 'We can't ever do this again, Rafe.' Her voice broke emotionally.

'Why the hell not?' he rasped his disappointment.

'I— We just can't!' Cairo cried, not even knowing how she was going to escape from this with dignity.

Minutes ago, she had been in ecstasy, totally lost to reason, but now she could see this for exactly what it was. A purely physical attraction—at least, on Rafe's part. Cairo was very much afraid that for her—as it had been eight years ago—it was something totally different.

She stared at Rafe, at his dark beauty, her eyes widening with horror as she realized that, despite everything, she was still in love with him.

Had she ever really stopped loving him?

No, she hadn't, Cairo acknowledged heavily. Rafe had been her first love and he was also her last love. But he hadn't been able to love her in return when they were together before, and it wasn't love he felt for her now, either. She had made a lot of mistakes in her life, but she wasn't about to make the biggest one of them all by deceiving herself into believing it could ever be otherwise!

She moved up and away from him to turn and pick up her discarded nightgown. 'I think it's time I went back inside. Alone,' she added abruptly so that Rafe should be left in no doubt about her intentions.

'Cairo?' Rafe stood up to reach out and grasp

her arm, turning her to face him as he looked down at her searchingly.

What the hell had just happened?

Minutes ago, he knew Cairo had been as wild for their lovemaking as he had, and now she was just going to walk away? He gave a puzzled shake of his head. 'What's going on, Cairo? Why are you so hot, so wild, one minute and then back to being the ice-maiden the next? Was I just a quick lay? Is that it?'

She gave a pained frown. 'It wasn't like that—'

'It sure as hell seems like it to me!' he grated.

She shrugged. 'I—I was curious, that's all.'

'You were *curious*?' he repeated in a dangerous tone.

She nodded. 'To see if that physical attraction really was still there.'

Rafe's eyes narrowed ominously. 'And?'

'Obviously it still is,' she acknowledged dryly. 'But that doesn't mean we have to do anything more about it.'

His mouth twisted derisively. 'Your *curiosity* has been satisfied. Is that it?'

'I— It was a mistake. A mistake that's better not repeated, don't you think?' Her face was very pale in the moonlight.

No, Rafe certainly did not think that!

Nor did he believe that Cairo was as coolly dismissive of what had just happened between them as she wanted him to believe. He just had no idea why she was behaving like this. With any other woman he would have said she was running scared from the depth of their response to each other, but he knew it couldn't be that because it had always been this way between them. From their very first night together their passion had been just this out of control.

'No, I don't think it was a mistake, and it's not what you really believe, either, Cairo,' he bit out.

She looked momentarily taken aback and then she gave an incredulous laugh. 'Strangely, Rafe, I find I don't actually give a damn *what* you think!'

'No?'

'No,' she insisted as she calmly slipped her night-gown back over her nakedness. 'It's only your own arrogance that makes you say differently.'

'You—' Rafe swallowed an angry expletive. 'You're playing with fire, Cairo,' he warned harshly.

'But that's my point, Rafe; I have played, and I don't want to play any more.' She shrugged. 'Maybe Lionel was right, after all, and my tastes have become more—sophisticated, over the years. I certainly hope I've learnt never to make the same mistake twice,' she added.

Rafe drew in an angry breath. 'Let's hope you've learnt the same sense where Bond is concerned, then,' he snarled.

'What's this got to do with Lionel?'

Rafe's mouth twisted humourlessly. 'Unless it escaped your notice earlier, the man obviously wants you back.'

'It isn't me Lionel wants, Rafe,' she contradicted.

'What do you mean?' he prompted sharply.

'Never mind.' Cairo gave a weary sigh. 'It really is very late, Rafe, and despite her late night I'm sure Daisy will still be awake bright and early in the morning.'

Rafe looked at her searchingly for several long seconds, a gaze that Cairo returned unblinkingly. Unemotionally. The passionate woman he had held in his arms such a short time ago had completely disappeared behind that façade of cool indifference.

But to Rafe it was obvious now that it *was* just a façade and he was more determined than ever to penetrate it. For now, though, he knew Cairo had had enough. Of Lionel Bond. And of him. If he tried to push her any more tonight, she would just retreat even further behind that barrier she had erected around her emotions.

He forced the tension from his shoulders and smiled slightly. 'Okay, Cairo.' He nodded. 'Sleep well, hmm?' he added ruefully—knowing he wasn't going to be as lucky!

She looked a little less certain as she eyed him guardedly. 'I— Yes. And you.'

He grimaced. 'I think I'll go for another swim and cool off.'

'Goodnight, then.'

''Night, Cairo,' he echoed huskily.

Rafe stood and watched her as she glided up the steps before disappearing inside the villa.

He stood there for several more minutes and mulled over this last conversation with Cairo, wondering exactly what she had meant by that last remark about Lionel Bond....

CHAPTER NINE

'NICE of you to join us,' Rafe drawled dryly as Cairo stepped onto the terrace where he and Daisy were eating breakfast.

'Good morning, Daisy.' Cairo completely ignored Rafe's jibe as she sat down next to her niece and poured herself a cup of coffee. 'I knew you were up,' she told him as she sat back in her chair cradling her mug of black coffee. 'I heard you and Daisy talking hours ago.'

'Was that before or after we went out and got breakfast?' Rafe taunted as he helped himself to another of the freshly baked croissants.

'Does it matter?' Cairo asked airily.

She had been woken by Daisy's overloud whispers at least two hours ago, Rafe's equally audible replies telling Cairo that her niece wasn't alone, and so she had simply pulled the duvet back over her head and gone back to sleep!

She gave a contented sigh as she gazed out at the tranquillity of the valley. 'It's another lovely day.'

'We're going home today, Aunty Cairo!' Daisy could obviously contain her excitement no longer.

Cairo raised questioning brows at Rafe before giving her niece a quizzical smile. 'We are…?'

Daisy nodded, her eyes glowing and her cheeks flushed. 'I wanted to come and wake you hours ago so I could tell you, but Uncle Rafe wouldn't let me disturb you.'

'What I actually said, Daisy, was that women of your aunt's advanced age need all the beauty sleep they can get!' Rafe corrected mockingly.

Cairo had wondered just how she and Rafe were going to face each other again after the incident down by the pool last night—now she knew! Sarcasm was obviously the order of the day….

She gave him a saccharin-sweet smile. 'And I thought we had agreed last night that, at the advanced age of thirty-seven, it's you who needs your beauty sleep?' That Rafe looked very lean and dangerously attractive in a white T-shirt and faded jeans gave lie to that statement!

Daisy turned to look at Rafe, her eyes wide. 'Are you really thirty-seven, Uncle Rafe?'

Rafe gave a rueful nod of his head in Cairo's direction as he heard the note of awe in Daisy's voice. 'Daisy, honey, when you're older, you'll realize that men are like a fine wine—they just get better as they mature.'

'Or they become as sour as vinegar,' Cairo put in lightly.

And not exactly honestly, where Rafe was concerned, she acknowledged inwardly. He did have at least one thing in common with a fine wine, as last night testified only too well—the last eight years had just made him more headily potent!

He looked across at her with teasing blue eyes. 'I think your Aunty Cairo is—confusing her wines,' he drawled.

That was quite enough of that conversation, Cairo decided firmly. 'So, we're leaving later today…?' she prompted in a pointed attempt to change the subject.

Rafe continued to hold her gaze challengingly for several more seconds before nodding. 'Jeff telephoned earlier; Margo and baby Simon are going to be discharged tomorrow morning.'

Cairo's face lit up and she put her coffee mug down on the table so that she could give Daisy a hug. 'That's wonderful news!'

Rafe took advantage of Cairo's momentary distraction to take in her appearance. She looked sleek and tanned this morning in a knee-length cream sundress, her legs bare and silky. She had cream flip-flops on her feet, and her face was bare of make-up, too, apart from a peachy gloss she had applied to her lips.

The lips that still looked slightly bruised from the force of their lovemaking the previous evening….

His stomach muscles clenched. Dammit, he had promised himself he wouldn't think about last night! At least, not until after he had safely delivered Daisy back to Margo and Jeff, anyway….

Cairo was still smiling as she looked across the table at him. 'What travel arrangements have you made for Daisy and me?'

'For all three of us,' Rafe corrected.

Cairo's smile faded. 'But you can't leave yet—'

'I can do what I please, Cairo.' Rafe scowled.

'But what about the film festival?'

'What about it?'

Cairo shrugged. 'I assumed you needed to be there to collect your award.'

'*If* I win an award, my assistant director can pick it up,' Rafe dismissed without concern. 'It's more important to get you and Daisy back to England.'

'I'm quite capable of getting myself and Daisy back to England, thank you very much—'

'I have a private jet organized to fly us out this afternoon,' he cut in abruptly in a tone that brooked no argument.

Cairo frowned as she slowly released Daisy. 'But I came over in my car....'

'I've also made arrangements for your car to be collected and driven back to England.'

Her brows rose at his arrogance. 'I really would rather drive my own car back, *if* you don't mind.'

'I don't mind in the least,' Rafe drawled. 'But

you might want to look at these before making a definite decision on that…' He pushed a pile of newspapers across the table towards her.

Cairo glanced down at the newspapers, her eyes widening as the very first one in the pile, an English publication, had a front-page photograph of herself and Rafe smiling at each other as they sat at the table together in the square in Grasse.

Cairo became very still as she pulled the tabloid newspaper further across the table. Although that hadn't been necessary in order to be able to read the three inch headline above the photograph: CAIRO AND RAFE FIND LOVE IN THE SOUTH OF FRANCE!

Not exactly subtle. But, then, were any of the tabloids?

'More photographs and story on page three' was the smaller announcement beneath that damning photograph.

What story? Cairo wondered incredulously. Until she and Rafe returned to the villa last night there hadn't been a story—

Oh, no…!

No!

Cairo could feel herself paling even as she quickly turned to page three, her breath leaving her in a relieved gasp as she saw that the 'story' actually only consisted of half a dozen more photographs of herself and Rafe together yesterday in Grasse.

'That man didn't take a single photograph of me, Aunty Cairo,' Daisy told her indignantly.

'Didn't he, love?' she answered distractedly as she moved on to the next newspaper in the pile.

This one, and the other four, all had photographs of herself and Rafe as they arrived at the party in Cannes together the previous evening.

Not a single one of those reporters had been enterprising enough to follow them back to the villa last night in the hopes of taking intimate photographs of her and Rafe together. Thank goodness!

She and Rafe looked good together, she realized with a fierce frown. With her wearing three inch heels they were of a similar height, Rafe's dark hair and swarthy skin a perfect foil for her own fairer colouring as they stood close together, Rafe's hand resting lightly beneath her elbow, a confident smile curving his lips.

Looks can be deceptive, Cairo decided firmly as she pushed the newspapers away to look across the table at the man himself. 'Your point is…?'

God, she was beautiful when she was being haughty, Rafe acknowledged admiringly. If a little lacking in perception! 'Surely it's obvious? You turn up anywhere today expecting to travel home by public transport and you're going to be mobbed by yet more reporters.'

'Damn!' She grimaced. 'Damn, damn, damn!'

Rafe relaxed back in his chair as he regarded her mockingly. 'Are you sure that's appropriate language to use in front of Daisy?'

'Daddy says *damn* isn't swearing, Uncle Rafe,' Daisy told him brightly. 'And neither is—'

'I think your daddy is using a lot of poetic licence, Daisy,' Rafe teased. 'Still not want to come on the plane with us this afternoon, Cairo?' He arched quizzical brows.

Cairo didn't want to go anywhere with Rafe, not this afternoon or at any other time! But neither was she stupid enough to turn down the offer when the alternative was sure to turn out to be the nightmare Rafe had just described.

She sighed with resignation. 'What time do you want us to be ready to leave?'

His eyes gleamed with satisfaction. 'Two o'clock should do it. We— Who the hell is that?' He scowled darkly as he stood up to glare down at the car driving up the private road to the villa.

Cairo stood up to stand beside him, a sinking feeling in the pit of her stomach as she thought she knew exactly who it was.

Either another enterprising reporter.

Or, more likely, it was Lionel…

He had left three messages on her mobile during the night. The first had been pleasant as he told her how nice it had been to see her again yesterday evening.

The second one had started out pleasant enough, too, with him asking her to meet with him so that they could talk. Unfortunately, as so often happened, it had deteriorated into insults after that as Lionel, obviously the worse for champagne, accused her of having been involved in an affair with Rafe all the time they had been married. As if! Cairo hadn't even been able to bear being on the same continent as Rafe for the last few years, let alone share the same bed after what he'd done to her.

Also predictably, the third message had been Lionel apologizing for the previous abusive one!

Cairo hadn't returned any of those calls. What was the point? She might still feel a certain amount of guilt where Lionel was concerned, had always felt that her lack of love for him had contributed to his addiction for gambling, but all the guilt in the world couldn't change the fact that they both knew their marriage was over.

'Do you want me to deal with this if it's another reporter?' Rafe asked grimly, turning to look at Cairo as she made no response.

She was staring intently at the car as it slowly came up the service road, her dark eyes shadowed above hollow cheeks.

'Cairo…?' he prompted.

She drew in a ragged breath before turning to

look at him. 'I— Would you mind taking Daisy down to the pool or something?' she muttered.

'Why on earth would I—'

'Because I think our visitor is Lionel, that's why,' she explained wearily.

Lionel Bond was coming *here*?

Rafe turned his attention back to the car, his gaze narrowed as he tried to identify person behind the wheel. Yep. It was Bond, all right.

He glanced down at Cairo. 'Do you want to speak to him?'

'Not particularly.' She grimaced.

'Then don't,' Rafe rasped.

She gave a wistful smile. 'It isn't as simple as that, Rafe.'

'Yes, Cairo.' Rafe nodded. 'It really is.'

She looked up at him quizzically. 'Maybe for you it is, Rafe.' She sighed. 'But I've never been able to be quite that cruel.'

He shrugged. 'Sometimes you have to be cruel to be kind,' he said curtly.

'Like you were with me eight years ago?' she challenged.

Rafe's mouth thinned at the accusation. 'I don't believe we were talking about you and me.'

'No, of course we weren't,' Cairo said immediately. 'Forget I said that.'

Rafe wasn't sure he wanted to forget it. He had been so stunned when Cairo had ended things between them so unexpectedly, quickly followed by her announcement of her engagement to Bond, that the two of them had never got to talk about the abrupt end of their own relationship.

Now probably wasn't the best time to have that talk, either….

'Okay, Cairo,' he acquiesced. 'Talk to Bond if that's what you feel you have to do. But at the first sign of trouble I'm coming back up here to knock his teeth down his throat!'

Cairo stared up at him for several seconds before she gave an incredulous laugh. 'I really don't think that will be necessary, Rafe, but thanks for the offer!'

'Believe me, it will be my pleasure.'

How strange that Rafe, of all people, should offer to be her protector, Cairo mused as she walked over to meet with Lionel in the driveway. Not that Cairo would ever ask for his help, but she could still appreciate the irony of the situation.

However, her rueful smile quickly faded to one of weary resignation as she approached Lionel. 'How much do you need this time, Lionel?' she asked heavily.

'So what did he want?'

Cairo turned from packing the suitcase open on top of her bed, her expression becoming guarded as she looked at Rafe as he leant against the door frame.

She straightened. 'I really don't think that's any of your business, Rafe.'

He raised an eyebrow. 'I think you'll find, Cairo, that I don't really care what you do or don't consider my business.'

Rafe had spent the last fifteen minutes beside the pool watching from behind dark sunglasses as Cairo and her ex-husband talked together on the terrace, trying to gauge from their body language exactly what was going on. But Cairo's ultra-calm demeanour and Bond's animated one hadn't really told him an awful lot.

He had expected Cairo to join him and Daisy beside the pool once the other man had got back in his car and left, but instead she had disappeared inside the villa.

To pack, it seemed…

'Well?' he prompted impatiently.

Cairo frowned. 'I'm sorry, Rafe, but I'm not telling you anything—' She broke off, her eyes widening as Rafe crossed the room in three long strides to stand just inches away from her. She swallowed hard. 'Shouldn't you be outside with Daisy?'

'Daisy's too excited about going home to swim any more and has gone to her room to dress, instead.'

Cairo had no intention of telling Rafe the reason for Lionel's visit. It was awkward enough that Lionel had tracked down the reporter from yesterday in order to find out where she was staying with Rafe, without going into the details of their conversation.

'Shouldn't you be packing, too, if we're leaving for the airport in a couple of hours?' she pointed out, inwardly wishing Rafe wouldn't stand quite this close to her; his proximity was totally unnerving her!

Rafe shook his head. 'I find Bond's visit much more interesting than packing.'

'Really?'

'Yes—really,' Rafe drawled. 'You made an intriguing comment yesterday evening…'

'Just the one?' she came back in mock disappointment. 'And here I was deceiving myself that I'm much more interesting than that!'

Rafe gave an admiring smile as he appreciated the way Cairo was trying to change the subject. But Rafe had no intention of letting her succeed.

'Oh, don't worry, you are *extremely* interesting,' he assured her throatily. 'But you implied last night that it isn't you Bond is interested in. So if it's not you, what is it?'

Her smile faded as her gaze became guarded. 'I really can't discuss this with you, Rafe—'

'Oh, but you really can, Cairo,' Rafe insisted softly, his own gaze compelling.

She shook her head. 'Not without breaking a confidence, I can't,' she told him determinedly.

Rafe's eyes widened. 'A confidence with *Bond*?' he murmured disbelievingly. 'You divorced the man three months ago!' he reminded her.

'Yes, I did,' she acknowledged stiffly. 'But that doesn't mean I have to actually hate him, does it? Or discuss his private business with someone he regards as—' She broke off, frowning.

'"He regards as"…?'

'Never mind,' Cairo said hurriedly. 'Lionel and I may be divorced, but I don't hate him,' she insisted.

Rafe grimaced. 'In my experience that's what usually happens when two people divorce.'

'Well, it isn't true in my case,' Cairo assured him firmly.

How could she possibly hate Lionel when she still felt so responsible for what had gone wrong between them? She couldn't. But without telling

Rafe the whole sorry story of her marriage, of the fact that she had married Lionel while still in love with *him*, she couldn't even begin to explain her feelings of guilt…

'I can see that,' Rafe grated harshly. 'Why bother to divorce him if you're going to come running every time the man crooks his little finger?'

Her eyes glittered darkly. 'It isn't like that!'

'Then what the hell *is* it like?' Rafe demanded incredulously. 'Last night you gave every impression that meeting Bond again was an ordeal for you, and yet today the two of you seem to have shared a pleasant conversation together!'

Cairo had found meeting Lionel again an ordeal because she had hoped—prayed—that when she ended their marriage, it might finally snap him into doing something about the mess his life had become. Those telephone calls last night, his visit today to ask her for money—yet again—told her that wasn't the case….

But without revealing everything to Rafe—which she had no intention of doing!—she was never going to persuade him of that. Lionel had managed to hide his gambling addiction from everyone for years, and Cairo certainly couldn't be the one to betray him now. Not even to convince Rafe that there was nothing between herself and Lionel.

Especially not in order to convince Rafe that there was nothing between herself and Lionel! Last night had shown her all too clearly just how dangerously susceptible she still was to Rafe….

'I really would prefer it if you stayed out of my life, Rafe.'

'And what if *I* would *prefer* to remain in it?' he challenged.

'This is ridiculous—'

'I agree,' Rafe interrupted.

Cairo scowled at him. 'Can we just stop playing word games?'

He raised dark brows. 'What other sort of games did you have in mind?'

She gave an impatient snort. 'I've never particularly liked playing games of any sort,' she snapped. 'Even as a child I was always the one that landed on the snake!'

Rafe gave an appreciative grin. 'I like you in this feisty mood, Cairo.'

'I don't want you to like me, Rafe!' she insisted as she moved away from him to resume her packing, but not as neatly as she had earlier, instead throwing things haphazardly inside the suitcase.

Rafe continued to look at her through narrowed lids for several long minutes.

She didn't seem overly upset by Lionel Bond's visit. More resigned than anything else.

But resigned to *what*?

CHAPTER TEN

'HE'S absolutely gorgeous, Margo!' Cairo told her sister warmly as she stood up to hand baby Simon back into his mother's arms.

They had left the villa and the South of France without further incident, arriving back in England in the early evening, with a car waiting there for them. Rafe had driven them all to the clinic to visit Margo. The proud father was there, too, of course, Jeff looking and sounding much more relaxed now that the danger was over for both Margo and the baby.

It certainly wasn't the time for Cairo to remonstrate with either of them for failing to tell her of Rafe's ownership of the villa and his subsequent surprise arrival!

Rafe had brought in Daisy's small suitcase so

that the little girl could return home with her father, leaving Cairo with the uncomfortable feeling he was going to insist on driving her to her flat. A feeling that was confirmed a short time later as he took his leave of Margo and Jeff at the same time as Cairo did, his hand firmly on her elbow as they walked down the carpeted corridor together.

'I'm sure you have somewhere else to go, Rafe, so—'

'Don't even think about trying to get rid of me just yet,' Rafe warned softly as he pushed the door open for her to go outside into the early evening sunshine. 'In fact, why don't the two of us go out to dinner? You weren't expecting to be back in England for several more days, so you won't have anything in your apartment for us to eat,' he reasoned.

Cairo frowned up at him as he unlocked the doors of the sporty black car. 'Despite what you seem to have assumed to the contrary, it was never my intention to have dinner with you this evening, either at my flat or anywhere else!'

He gave a mocking smile as he opened her door for her. 'That isn't very friendly of you, Cairo, after I've gone to the trouble of transporting you back to England so quickly and efficiently.'

'It wasn't just me, Rafe, you also transported yourself and Daisy back….'

'Ah, but as you pointed out earlier today, I really needed to stay in Cannes. I don't even have a hotel reservation for tonight yet…' He quirked dark brows at her.

Cairo glared at him. 'That's your problem, Rafe, not mine.'

'I'm sure you could make it yours, too, if you really wanted to….'

She stared at him in disbelief. Was Rafe actually *flirting* with her? It certainly seemed as if he was!

'But I really don't want to,' Cairo told him dryly. 'So could you either give me my suitcase from the boot of the car so that I can get a taxi home, or drive me there yourself?'

'I'm driving you there myself, of course,' Rafe stated.

Cairo continued to eye him suspiciously as she

slid into the passenger seat, not trusting him in this mood at all.

But what could he do, really? She didn't even have to invite him into her flat if—

There was no 'if' about it—she wasn't going to invite Rafe into her flat at all!

'Very nice,' Rafe murmured approvingly as he stood in the hallway looking at the simplicity of the sitting-room in Cairo's apartment, liking the cream carpet and terracotta-coloured suite, the paintings on the walls all bright and cheerful, too.

Cairo stood firmly in the doorway blocking his entrance to the room. 'Okay, Rafe, you've delivered my suitcase, as you insisted on doing,' she bit out, still irritated that she had lost that particular argument. 'Now it's time for you to leave.'

He put the case down. 'You could show your gratitude by offering me a glass of wine....'

Her foot tapped impatiently. 'I was quite capable of carrying my own suitcase!'

'I'm sure you're quite capable of doing most things yourself, Cairo, but my father brought me up to be a Spanish gentleman. And carrying a lady's bags for her is one of the things a Spanish gentleman does.'

Cairo wasn't fooled for a moment by this explanation; Rafe had been determined to wangle an invitation into her flat from the start. She just wasn't sure why....

'Very well.' She sighed heavily. 'Would you care for a glass of wine, Rafe?'

'How kind of you to offer, Cairo,' he accepted sarcastically, before stepping past her into the sitting-room.

Leaving Cairo no choice but to follow him! 'Red or white?' she offered, more than a touch disgruntled.

'Red would be fine, thanks. Have you lived here for very long?' he asked as he made himself comfortable in one of the armchairs.

'Six months or so,' Cairo answered distractedly as she took a bottle of red wine from the rack and uncorked it before pouring some of the wine into two glasses. 'Here.' She thrust one under Rafe's nose.

Blue eyes glinted with mockery as he looked up at her before taking the glass, his fingers lightly brushing against hers as he did so....

Cairo made no effort to sit down herself but instead walked over to look out of the window high above the London skyline as she slowly sipped her own wine, all the time aware of that intense blue gaze on the rigidity of her back.

'For goodness' sake, relax, Cairo.' Rafe finally sighed into the tense silence.

How was she supposed to do that when Rafe was in her flat?

This was *her* space, the first place she could completely call her own for over eight years. And Rafe's presence was a definite intrusion on that solitude.

'Nice view.'

Cairo almost dropped her glass of wine at the close proximity of Rafe's voice, turning to glare at him as he stood beside her, his tread having been so soft on the carpet she hadn't realized he had joined her in front of the window. 'I like it,' she snapped irritably.

'I'm not sure it's a good idea for you to be drinking on a relatively empty stomach,' Rafe commented; Cairo hadn't eaten any breakfast at all, and only a sandwich for lunch.

'The wine was *your* idea—'

'For you to offer me a glass,' he corrected. 'You know what happens if you drink wine and you haven't had enough to eat,' he reminded her huskily.

'I know what happened once, Rafe. Just once,' she reiterated firmly, the blush on her cheeks telling him she remembered the incident only too well.

'Hmm.'

'And what's that supposed to mean?' she challenged.

Rafe had forgotten what fun it was to tease Cairo. How she got that light of battle in her eyes. The angry blush to her cheeks. Her mouth set in that stubborn line.

He took the remaining half-glass of wine from her fingers and placed it on a bookshelf with his own. 'Come out to dinner with me tonight, Cairo,' he invited gruffly.

She blinked up at him uncertainly. 'Why on earth would I want to do that?' she breathed huskily, but with much less conviction in her voice.

Rafe held her gaze with his as he gave her a quizzical smile. 'Because I'm a stranger in town—'

'You're Rafe Montero—you could ask any woman to have dinner with you and she would drop anything else she had planned just to be there!'

'The one I'm asking right now doesn't have anything else planned—and yet she's refusing.'

'Rafe—'

'Cairo?'

'You really are—' She broke off frustratedly. '*Why* do you want me to have dinner with you?'

He shrugged. 'Because we both have to eat this evening and we may as well do it together.'

She shook her head. 'If you think, because of what happened last night, that I'm going to sleep with you later, then—'

'Cairo, the invitation was for dinner, not bed,' he cut in firmly.

'Yes...' She eyed him suspiciously.

'Although I doubt I would be averse to the idea later on if you were to—'

'I won't!'

He raised an eyebrow. 'Then I guess I'll settle for dinner.'

She sighed. 'Okay, Rafe, I'll come out to dinner with you. But only,' she continued as he would have smiled, 'if you promise me never to mention that embarrassing incident with the wine ever again.'

'You mean, the incident where you threw off all your clothes and—'

'Yes—that incident!' she glared.

'Fine.' It was difficult for Rafe to hold the smile back this time. 'I promise I'll never—ever—mention that night we had dinner in my hotel room eight years ago and you stripped off and tipped cream all over your—well, all over you—and then offered yourself as dessert—' He broke off, laughing now when Cairo began to pummel his chest with her fists, and was still grinning even as he held both her hands in his. 'It was the best dessert I ever had,' he told her throatily.

It was very hard to remain annoyed with him when he gave her that heart-melting smile, Cairo thought in despair. Especially when she also remembered the night in question—how could she ever forget it? It was the most wildly erotic night....

Which meant it also wasn't a good idea to let Rafe continue to hold her hands in his. Or to look into those sky-blue eyes that seduced her with only a glance. Or to allow him to draw her, slowly, purposefully, towards him—

'No, Rafe!' She broke that seductive spell as she straightened away from him, pulling her hands out of his grasp as she did so. 'I said dinner and I meant just dinner!'

'Pity,' he murmured lazily.

She gave him a reproving look. 'If you would like to sit here and finish your wine, I just need to go to my room to freshen up before we go out.'

Although she'd agreed to the lesser of two evils—going out to a restaurant with Rafe rather than having him stay on here—it still wasn't a good idea, Cairo told herself as she shut her bedroom door firmly behind her and leant back against it.

What game was Rafe playing now?

Whatever it was, she couldn't allow it to continue!

'How on earth did you manage to get a table here at such short notice— No, don't tell me.' Cairo gave a wry smile. 'You're *Rafe Montero*.'

Rafe studied her across the table in what was a very exclusive London restaurant. 'I really wish you wouldn't say my name as if it's some sort of expletive,' he drawled ruefully. 'Besides,' he continued lightly, 'there has to be some compensation to losing every vestige of your privacy just because you chose acting as a career.'

Cairo gave him a considering look, coolly beautiful in the green figure-hugging, knee-length dress she had changed into after freshening-up, her red hair long and silky. 'I never realized it bothered you.'

He shrugged. 'It wasn't a problem when we were on the Isle of Man. Since the film studio opened up there in the late nineties the islanders have become used to celebrities walking down Strand Street, and they pretty well take it in their stride. Most other places it can be a problem, though. That's the reason exclusive restaurants like this one are so popular with people like you and me. Everyone's a celebrity, so no one stares.'

No, Cairo acknowledged, no one was staring. Now. But the two of them had caused quite a stir when they'd arrived together half an hour ago, probably because of all the publicity about them in the English newspapers this morning....

Rafe gave her a quizzical glance. 'Do you ever regret becoming so well known?'

Did she? She could quite well have done without all the publicity that had surrounded her separation and divorce the last ten months. But otherwise...? No, probably not.

'It goes with the job, I suppose,' she said, before taking a sip of the pink champagne Rafe had ordered. A drink he had first introduced her to on the Isle of Man...

'And do you enjoy the job as much as you thought you would?'

'Sorry?' It was impossible for Cairo to miss the slight edge that had entered his tone.

Rafe shrugged. 'When you were twenty, you were pretty determined to make a name for yourself. At any price, apparently,' he added bitterly.

She put her champagne glass carefully back down on the table. 'Rafe, if you're going to start being insulting again, then I shall have to leave.'

'I've always assumed your ambition was the reason you married Bond so quickly and moved to the States with him.' He sat back in his chair, his gaze hooded as he looked across the table at her. 'Although I still have no idea why you agreed to talk to him when he came to the villa…' he added speculatively.

Cairo's mouth tightened. 'Rafe, you either desist in pursuing this subject or I *will* leave!'

'I'm just interested, Cairo,' he said. 'After all, we have to talk about something while we eat,' he added lightly as their first course was brought to the table.

Cairo waited until the waiter had left before answering Rafe. 'I do not want to talk about Lionel. Not his visit to the villa yesterday or anything to do with my marriage and divorce.' Unless Rafe wanted her to end up with indigestion! 'Why don't we discuss why it is you've never married, instead?' she added challengingly as she picked up her fork and began to eat her prawns.

Rafe smiled. 'I already told you, that's much less interesting.'

'Because you've never met the right woman,' Cairo taunted. 'And do you really believe that there's a right woman or right man for everyone?'

'Don't you?' Rafe had believed at one time that he had found the right woman for him. But, as it had turned out, he obviously hadn't been the right man for her….

Cairo shook her head. 'I think it's probably wiser—safer—to opt to be with someone of a similar background, career and interests.'

'Like you and Bond, you mean?'

Colour warmed her cheeks. 'Rafe—'

'Or you and me,' he added softly.

No, *not* like her and Rafe! As Cairo had learnt to her cost, she and Rafe had ultimately had absolutely nothing in common. Except a physical awareness that Cairo could feel even now....

Because no matter how she might try to deny it—to ignore it!—last night had only increased her awareness of everything about Rafe, from the silky glossiness of his hair down to the slender elegance of his feet.

She put her fork back down on her plate, her appetite having completely deserted her. 'No, not like you and me,' she denied huskily. 'I think it's time that I left, Rafe—'

'Run away, you mean?' he bit out caustically.

Her eyes flashed darkly. 'I'm *not* running away.'

'Sure you are. It's what you do—it's what you've always done,' he said grimly.

Her throat tightened painfully. 'I should have known your earlier pleasantness wouldn't last.'

'Because you obviously prefer a man with no ba—'

'How dare you?' Cairo gasped.

'How dare I?' Rafe repeated harshly. 'Oh, I think you'll find that where you're concerned I *dare* to do a lot of things— No, Cairo!' He sat forward to place his hand firmly over hers as she went to pick up her evening bag from the table before leaving. 'If you leave now, the headlines in tomorrow's newspapers are going to read, "Cairo and Rafe split up after only two days together".'

'We've never been together—'

'I remember a time when we were *very* together,' he growled.

'I—'

'Don't even think about denying what we once had, Cairo,' he warned.

'What I thought we had,' she corrected tightly.

'I thought we had it, too,' he rasped. 'You must have realized this last two days that I still want you—'

'Rafe, please don't—'

'And you still want me,' he added softly.

'I most certainly do not!' Her face blushed revealingly even as she spoke the lie. For how could Rafe ever doubt that she still wanted him after their lovemaking last night?

His mouth twisted humourlessly. 'Don't make me prove it, Cairo.'

The passionate heat in the blue of his eyes held her captive, the tension between them unbearable. She was barely breathing. Couldn't think. Couldn't speak. Was held in the glitter of that blue gaze like a fawn mesmerized by the headlights of an approaching car.

Because, amazingly, Rafe *was* approaching her! Completely unconcerned with their surroundings, and the other diners, he stood up, reached across the table and curved a hand beneath her chin to tilt her face up to his and place his mouth forcefully down on hers.

To claim.

To possess.

To totally steal Cairo's breath away as she felt herself responding to the hard demand of Rafe's mouth on hers.

Rafe's eyes glittered with emotion when he

finally raised his head to look down at her. 'I want to sweep everything off this table before laying you down on it and—' He broke off suddenly as they were surrounded by a soft round of appreciative applause, closing his eyes briefly before straightening to turn and give a brief, ironic bow to the diners who were smiling at the two of them indulgently. 'Scrap that previous headline,' he muttered as he resumed his seat. '"Cairo and Rafe can't keep their hands off each other" would probably be more appropriate!'

Cairo was dumbstruck, totally stunned by the unexpectedness of Rafe's kiss.

And by her own aching response....

Because for the time that Rafe's mouth had possessed hers she had totally forgotten their surroundings, would probably have helped him sweep the plates and glasses from the table-top before pulling him down on it and making love with him!

'How could you?' she finally gasped shakily, a brief, embarrassed glance around the restaurant telling her that the other diners—having obviously enjoyed the show!—had now gone back to their own meals and conversation. 'That was absolutely— Rafe, how could you?' she said again.

It was more a question of how could he not, Rafe realised as he picked up his glass and took a much-needed swallow of the champagne. The challenge thrown down, he simply hadn't been able to stop himself.

The problem was that Cairo made him forget everything else but her.

Being with her.

Making love with her.

And he still did want to make love with her— desperately; his body was hard and aching with that need right now. But one glance at Cairo's pale, accusing face told him that was as likely to happen, following that very public display, as snow in August!

Although surely it had to snow somewhere in the world in August….

His mouth twisted into a humourless smile. 'Perhaps we should just put it down to your own fatalistic allure.'

Cairo glared at him. 'And perhaps we should just put it down to your need to humiliate me!'

Rafe winced. 'Cairo—'

'Don't bother trying to deny it, Rafe, because you know that's exactly what you did.' She picked up her bag, her face flushed with anger now, and her eyes glittering darkly. 'I think we'll just stick with the original headline, hmm?' With one last fiercely scathing glance she stood up and left the table, her head held high as she made her way through the restaurant to where the maître d' held the door open for her leave.

Well, that certainly went well, Rafe, he congratulated himself dourly as he threw the rest of the champagne in his glass to the back of his throat before refilling it. The chances of Cairo now letting him anywhere near her again, let alone making love with her, were once more as likely as that snow in August!

Not good enough odds, Rafe decided as he threw some money down on the table to pay for their meal before following Cairo, his expression grim.

CHAPTER ELEVEN

RAFE caught up with Cairo as she stood on the pavement outside trying to flag down an available cab, something apparently not that easy to find since the new regulation banning the use of private cars from the inner city roads had increased the demand.

'Would it help if I apologized?'

Cairo glanced round sharply at the sound of Rafe's voice behind her, then glared at him in the semi-darkness. 'Not in the least,' she informed him coldly, before turning back to look for a taxi with its light on, at the same time completely aware of the fact that Rafe had moved to stand beside her.

'Cairo, at least let me drive you home—'

'And give you the chance to humiliate me yet

again?' she snapped. 'I'd rather walk!' She began to do exactly that.

Rafe fell into step beside her. 'Cairo, you still haven't had hardly anything to eat—'

'And whose fault is that?' she accused as she came to an abrupt halt, positively bristling with anger at him. 'I went out to dinner with you in the first place completely against my better judgement—and look how right my reservations proved to be!' She gave an impatient shake of her head. 'Just face it, Rafe, you and I have absolutely nothing left to say to each other.'

Rafe totally disagreed; the amount of things they had never said to each other would fill a football stadium!

He drew in a ragged breath. 'We used to be able to communicate without words—'

'Is that what all this is about, Rafe?' she challenged. 'If all you want is to go to bed with me again, then why don't you just say so?' Her breasts quickly rose and fell in her agitation.

Because it *wasn't* all he wanted, dammit! But quite what he *did* want Rafe wasn't sure of, either—yet. The only thing he did know, now that he had spent time with Cairo again, was that he wasn't willing to let another eight years pass before he saw or spoke to her again.

'And if it is?' he rasped.

She stared at him for several tense seconds. 'Fine,' she finally said. 'Let's go back to my flat and have sex, then, shall we?' She turned back in the direction Rafe had parked the car.

Rafe stood unmoving, a frown creasing his brow.

He did want Cairo. He wanted to make slow, leisurely love to her again. But not like this. Never like this.

She stopped several feet away to turn back and face him, auburn brows raised in mocking query. 'Changed your mind, Rafe?' she taunted.

He shook his head. 'This isn't like you, Cairo—'

'I thought we had agreed that you don't really know me!' she scorned. 'Last chance, Rafe,' she added. 'A once-in-a-lifetime offer!' Her eyes glittered.

Not with anger, but with tears, Rafe recognized with horror.

Cairo knew she was almost at breaking point. That much more of this conversation and she was going to end up blubbering like a complete idiot. Which was ridiculous. She was a twenty-eight-year-old recently divorced woman, for goodness' sake; most women in her position would have been only too happy to be offered a night of uncomplicated sex with Rafe Montero!

Except Cairo wasn't 'most women' and, loving Rafe as she now knew she still did, it wouldn't be just uncomplicated sex to her, either….

'Time's up, I'm afraid,' she announced with faux brightness as Rafe still made no response to her offer. 'You had your chance and you—' She broke off suddenly as Rafe stepped forward to wrap his arms about her and hold her against him with a gentleness that was completely her undoing.

A sob caught at the back of Cairo's throat as she allowed her head to drop forward onto Rafe's shoulder and the tears began to fall hotly down her cheeks. Then his arms tightened about her as she began to cry in earnest.

'I'm sorry, Cairo,' he groaned into her hair. 'I am *so* sorry!'

Rafe's apology—for what exactly…?—just made her cry all the harder, deep, racking tears that she hadn't allowed to fall during the last ten months. Probably because she had known that once she started she wouldn't be able to stop!

The tears fell like a river now, completely drenching the front of Rafe's shirt as he continued to hold her.

She cried for the loss of Rafe eight years ago.

She cried for her years of being married to Lionel.

She cried for the end of that marriage.

She cried for the loneliness that was so deep inside her it threatened to completely overwhelm her.

But finally there were no more tears left, and instead Cairo became aware of exactly where she was—and in whose arms she was crying.

Rafe Montero's.

The man who had so cruelly broken her heart eight years ago, and had so unwittingly—uncaringly?—shaped those intervening years….

She began to extricate herself from his arms, brushing the tears from her cheeks as she straightened, her gaze avoiding his as she pushed her hair back behind her ears. 'Well, that was a little—embarrassing, wasn't it?' She gave a broken laugh, frowning as she saw the lip gloss smeared across the front of Rafe's now very damp white shirt. 'I'm sorry about that.' She brushed ineffectually at the smear before stepping back. 'If it doesn't come out in the wash let me know and I'll replace the shirt—'

'Cairo.'

'It's silk, right?' Cairo continued. 'Although you'll have to tell me your size, I'm afraid—'

'Cairo.'

'I've never been very good at guessing a man's shirt size. I remember I once—'

'Cairo, just *stop*, will you?' Rafe cut in forcefully, a dark scowl on his brow.

Her gaze was guarded as she looked up at him,

her eyes red and puffy from the tears she had cried, her cheeks blotchy and her nose slightly red for the same reason.

She had never looked more beautiful to Rafe….

After an interminable pause, she finally murmured warily, 'Unless it's escaped your notice, Rafe, I have stopped now.'

He gave a rueful smile. 'I noticed.'

She frowned slightly. 'And…?'

'You really do need to eat this evening, so how about we pick up a Chinese takeaway on the way back to your apartment?' He shrugged. 'It's the least I can do after behaving so badly I made you miss dinner,' he added persuasively as her eyes widened. 'We can make it a Chinese takeaway for one, if that's what you would prefer?' he offered as Cairo continued to look at him suspiciously.

'If we make it a meal for two, what happens afterwards?'

Rafe's mouth tightened. 'Afterwards I'll leave,' he said curtly. 'Hell, Cairo, just because I don't have someone in my life at the moment doesn't mean I spend my every waking hour trying to devise ways of getting you into bed!' he added as she still hesitated.

Well, not his *every* waking hour…but Rafe had to admit—to himself, at least!—that he hadn't thought of too much else since arriving at the villa two days ago and finding Cairo there, and it had got even worse since their stormy love-making the previous evening.

'I didn't imagine that you did,' she said dryly.

He quirked dark brows. 'No?'

'No!'

'Okay, then,' Rafe said. 'So do we get Chinese food for one or two?'

She needed her head examined, Cairo knew, to even be thinking of prolonging this evening with Rafe. And yet she *was* thinking about it….

No doubt the two of them would end up arguing again before the evening was over. They seemed to do little else nowadays. And yet Cairo still felt a certain reluctance to say a final goodbye to him….

'Two,' she decided at last. 'I'll probably have cause to regret that, too, but—'

'You never did know quite when to stop talking,' Rafe remarked as they began to walk back to the car.

Her eyes narrowed. 'I'm already starting to regret it—'

'Please just get in the car, Cairo,' he instructed as he opened the passenger door for her, having no intention of arguing with her again before they had eaten.

No doubt it would be another matter afterwards!

'So you're going back to work, after all? And in the theatre?' Rafe couldn't hide his surprise as the two of them sat on the carpeted floor in the sitting-room of Cairo's apartment using chopsticks to eat the Chinese food directly from the cartons, and finishing off the bottle of red wine Cairo had opened earlier.

Cairo had suggested warming plates and laying the table, but Rafe had vetoed the idea, opting for this less formal way of dining once Cairo had changed into comfortable worn jeans and a green cashmere sweater so that she could sit cross-legged on the floor.

'I start rehearsals in a little under two weeks and open in three.' Cairo nodded as she reached over to pick up a prawn.

Rafe found himself watching as she lifted the chopsticks and deftly popped the food into her mouth, her lips bare of gloss—well, they would be, as most of it was still on his shirt!

He had always loved Cairo's mouth. The fullness of her lips. The way they tilted slightly at the corners. Their pouting softness when he kissed them....

'I'm really looking forward to it,' she added, before licking the sauce from those delectable lips.

Rafe dragged his gaze away, aware that it was only the way he was also sitting cross-legged on the carpet that prevented Cairo from seeing his purely physical response to the provocation that was her mouth.

He nodded. 'I remember you saying years ago that it was your first love. But it's hard work, and there's no money in it—'

'I'm not interested in the money, Rafe.' Cairo turned to him impatiently. 'I want the immediacy of the theatre. The audience response as each performance is just slightly different. The adrenalin rush each night just before you step onto the stage for the first time.' She shook her head, her eyes glowing. 'There's nothing quite like it.'

Rafe could see that for Cairo there wasn't.

His own years of performing off-Broadway, before he was 'discovered' by a movie producer, seemed like a lifetime ago, but he did still remember that adrenalin rush.

He was just surprised, that after years of starring in increasingly popular box-office hits—the millions Cairo was paid for each performance increasing as a result—she was actually going back to the gruelling demand of theatre work with very little monetary reward.

'Maybe I'll come to your opening night…' he murmured.

Cairo gave him a sharp glance. 'What on earth for?'

He tensed. 'Why not?'

Admittedly this last hour of just sitting on the floor, eating informally and chatting about everything and nothing—mainly nothing, as it was less controversial!—had been very pleasant after the previously fraught forty-eight hours.

But the last thing Cairo needed was to know that Rafe was sitting out in the audience on the first night of her return to the theatre after a break of almost eight years.

What if she was awful?

Making films was totally different from working on stage—no retakes for one thing!—and Cairo was nervous enough already without the added pressure of knowing Rafe was sitting beyond the footlights watching her.

'I would really rather you didn't, Rafe.' She grimaced.

He frowned his irritation. 'Why the hell not?' he repeated harshly.

Well, Cairo supposed it would have been too much to expect 'very pleasant' to last for too much longer!

She sat back. 'Why would you want to bother? Just so that you can see me fall flat on my face?'

'That's damned unfair, Cairo, and you know it!' Rafe protested.

'No, I don't know it, Rafe.' Cairo shook her head. 'We aren't really even friends any more, so why on earth would you want to come to the theatre to watch me on my opening night?'

His eyes were glacial. 'Maybe I would just like to wish you well?'

'A bouquet of flowers would do that, don't you think?'

No, Rafe didn't. He found himself annoyed far beyond reason by Cairo's dismissal of his suggestion. Dammit, he wanted to come to London in three weeks' time and watch her opening performance!

She looked about eighteen again, sitting there in her tight jeans and that soft green sweater, her face almost bare of make-up, her hair pulled up into a band at her crown, leaving the long arch of her neck vulnerably bare.

Rafe's anger faded as quickly as it had flared into life. 'Are yellow roses still your favourite flowers?' he asked huskily.

Cairo gave him a startled look. 'I— Yes. Yes, they are.'

His mouth twisted self-derisively. 'You thought I'd forgotten.'

'I—' She broke off to once again moisten the pout of her lips with the tip of her tongue. 'It's been eight years, Rafe,' she pointed out.

Eight or eighty, Rafe hadn't forgotten a single thing about this woman's likes and dislikes. Either in bed or out of it!

She gave him a teasing smile. 'A lot of other women have passed through your—'

'Cairo,' Rafe bit out warningly.

'—life, since then,' she continued ruefully.

Rafe held her gaze with his as he reached over and plucked the chopsticks from her un-resisting fingers. 'And I couldn't tell you the fa-vourite flower of a single one of them,' he admitted softly.

Cairo blinked, totally disorientated by the way the atmosphere between them had once again changed from being charged with anger to sexual tension instead.

She shook her head as she nervously moistened her lips—

'Don't *do* that, Cairo!' Rafe groaned.

'Don't do what?' She was barely breathing as Rafe's head slowly bent towards hers.

'This,' he murmured throatily as his tongue stroked softly against her lips, lightly, erotically, igniting a warmth deep in the pit of Cairo's stomach as Rafe continued the caress.

Cairo closed her eyes as she gave herself up to the sensation, to that heat spreading to her thighs and causing her breasts to swell in tingling awareness as Rafe's tongue now dipped temptingly between her parted lips.

She groaned low in her throat as Rafe's lips slowly sipped and tasted hers and he pulled her closer against the hardness of his chest. Cairo's hands moved up of their own volition so that she could entangle her fingers in the dark thickness of his hair as he deepened the kiss to one of hungry demand.

Rafe had no idea how long he and Cairo kissed, deeply, hungrily, her breasts pressed against him as one of his hands moved beneath the softness of her sweater to caress the length of her spine from her nape to the dipping hollow at its base, her skin like silky velvet beneath his touch.

But it wasn't enough; he needed to kiss that velvety skin, too, wanted to cup her breasts in his hands and worship them with his lips and tongue until he heard those little noises in Cairo's throat that told him she was about to explode.

Dammit, he wished at that moment that he had the petals of dozens of yellow roses to scatter over the carpet before laying Cairo's naked body down on them as he parted her thighs and plunged his aching arousal inside their moist heat!

But instead, as Rafe attempted to lie down on the carpet with her, he found himself—and Cairo—surrounded by the smell and cartons of half-eaten Chinese food!

His mouth left hers and he raised his head to look at the offending cartons. 'Hell!' he muttered in frustration.

'I don't suppose chicken chow mein has the same appeal as whipped cream, does it?'

Rafe turned slowly back to look at Cairo, a smile curving his own lips as he saw the gleam of laughter in her eyes. 'We could try it, I suppose…'

'No, we could not!' Cairo protested laughingly as she turned on her side away from the food, taking Rafe with her so that she now lay on his chest. 'That's disgusting!' She shuddered just at the thought of those rapidly cooling noodles against her skin, slowly sobering as she found herself now looking down at Rafe, his eyes warm with intent. 'I'm not sure this is a good idea, Rafe,' she breathed.

He raised a hand to curve it about her cheek as his thumb moved caressingly against her lower lip. 'Live dangerously,' he encouraged.

That maybe wasn't such a good idea, either, when she had just spent the last eight years living with the repercussions of the last time she had acted so impulsively!

'Cairo, you think too much…' Rafe groaned as he obviously saw her uncertainty.

'First I talk too much, and now I think too much, too?'

'Sometimes you do, yes—'

'Well, one of us needs to, don't you think?' she asked tensely.

'You're deliberately trying to provoke an argument,' he said slowly. 'Why is that, Cairo? Why do you need to keep putting me at a distance?'

'You're hardly at a distance at this moment!' Her breasts were pressed against the hardness of his chest, her legs lying between his, the hardness of his arousal straining against her own heated thighs….

But the mood was broken, along with that tenuous link between them that had temporarily allowed Cairo to forget all the reasons why she should not allow herself to be here like this with Rafe.

'I'm not trying to provoke an argument.' She rolled away from him to sit up with her arms wrapped about her bent knees. 'I just don't want to make another mistake where you're concerned,' she explained.

Rafe sat up slowly, his gaze deliberately holding hers. 'I don't believe we were a mistake the first time around.'

She shrugged. 'You're entitled to your opinion, of course.'

His eyes narrowed. 'Exactly why did you finish things between us before, Cairo?'

She gave an impatient shake of her head. 'Isn't it a little bit late for the two of us to be having this conversation?'

'It's certainly long overdue, I would have thought,' he grated.

She sighed. 'You know exactly why I stopped seeing you.'

'You wanted to marry Bond—'

'You and I had parted before I so much as went out to dinner with him!' she defended herself heatedly.

'You broke up with me at lunchtime and went out with Bond the same evening!' Rafe's voice rose, too. 'I went shopping that morning and when the two of us met up for lunch, you told me that you didn't want to see me any more, that you needed to be free to concentrate on your career!' He scowled. 'Considering you went out with Bond that same evening, got engaged to him three days later, and then married him three weeks after that, your concentration must have been incredible!'

Cairo gasped at the insult. 'Don't try and turn this around on *me*, Rafe.'

'Who else am I supposed to blame?'

'I should try looking at your affair with Pamela Raines, if I were you!' she accused as she stood up to pace the room restlessly. 'You even spent the afternoon of my wedding in bed with her!'

Rafe scowled darkly. 'Well, I was hardly going to attend the wedding and wish you well, now, was—' He broke off to give her a narrow-eyed look. 'How the hell do you know how I spent that afternoon?'

Cairo glared at him. 'How do you think I know?'

'I have no idea—' He stopped and looked at her disbelievingly. '*Pamela* told you?'

Cairo nodded. 'It was the excuse she gave

when she arrived extremely late and dishevelled to the wedding reception, yes.'

Rafe shook his head. 'I can't believe she would— Why on earth did she do that?'

For the same reason the other woman had told Cairo three weeks previously that she and Rafe had been having an affair for weeks—because it was the truth!

That morning Rafe claimed to have gone shopping, Cairo had finished filming early and decided to go to Rafe's hotel suite, only to have the door opened—shockingly!—by a completely nude Pamela Raines, her hair rumpled, the bedclothes in disarray on the bed in the room behind her. Pamela's sympathy had been unbearable as she'd told Cairo that Rafe had been trying to tell her about the two of them for days now, but that he knew she was in love with him and was worried about how she would react if he told her about himself and Pamela, that he feared she might do something stupid.

Cairo had saved him the trouble and broken things off with him instead!

Calmly.

Coolly.

And then she *had* done something totally stupid!

Lionel had been asking Cairo to have dinner with him for several weeks, ever since his arrival in London to see how filming was going, and when he'd asked Cairo out again later that same afternoon, she had accepted. Still in the same reckless 'I'll show Rafe' state of mind, she had also accepted Lionel's whirlwind marriage proposal only three days later….

Cairo frowned now. 'I would really rather not talk about your affair with Pamela any more, Rafe—'

'There was *no* affair, dammit!' he rasped. 'I did spend the afternoon of your wedding in bed with Pamela, yes, but it was the first and last time—'

'It had been going on for weeks before my wedding!' Cairo accused, her voice rising agitatedly.

'What? Cairo, I categorically did *not* have an affair with Pamela Raines before your wedding!' Rafe scowled.

'She tells a completely different story!'

Rafe eyed her uncertainly now. 'She does?'

'Yes! Now will you please leave, Rafe?' she requested tautly. 'This whole conversation is giving me a headache.'

Rafe looked at her searchingly. The frown between her eyes, the strain he could see in reflected those dark brown eyes, the hollows of her pale cheeks, and the thin, unhappy line of her mouth, confirmed that she did indeed have a headache.

But he couldn't just leave it there. 'Cairo, you have to believe me—'

'Rafe, I don't *have* to do anything where you're concerned,' she cut in. 'I make it a policy never to talk about the past,' she added firmly as he would have spoken again. 'It serves no purpose but to open up old wounds—'

'What if those wounds never healed in the first place?' he asked.

She gave a derisive smile. 'I'm sorry to disappoint you, Rafe, but I was over you long ago.'

'I wasn't referring to *your* wounds, Cairo....'

Cairo became very still as she now looked at Rafe as searchingly as he had looked at her seconds ago.

He looked grim and determined, with an underlying impatience—he certainly didn't look anywhere near as devastated, or broken-hearted, as she had been that morning eight years ago when she'd discovered he was having an affair with Pamela Raines.

And all the talking in the world couldn't change that!

'It's far too late for the two of us to talk about this, Rafe,' she insisted. 'I have my own life now, and you have yours—and those lives have no common ground,' she said with certainty.

'We still want each other—'

'You're talking about sex again, Rafe,' Cairo interrupted. 'And, yes, I admit, having met you again, that it's interesting to realize the sexual attraction is still there,' she conceded. 'But the truth of the matter is I don't want any sort of relationship in my life right now, sexual or otherwise,' she added coldly.

The absolute certainty in her tone told Rafe that Cairo meant exactly what she was saying.

Which left him precisely where?

As far as Cairo was concerned, obviously nowhere.

But that didn't mean Rafe didn't intend finding out for himself exactly what had happened to the two of them all those years ago. Because one thing this conversation with Cairo had definitely told him was that there were things about that time he had been completely unaware of. Not that any of that was going to change how Cairo now felt about him, but *he* wanted—no, needed—to know, dammit!

He drew in a deep breath. 'This is goodbye, then, Cairo.'

'It would appear so, yes,' she clipped.

He gave a rueful smile. 'Friends usually kiss each other goodbye, don't they?'

Cairo gave a tight smile. 'I thought the one thing we had just agreed on was that the two of us can never be friends.'

Rafe shook his head. 'You can't seriously

believe that I mean to never see you again?' Just the thought of that happening made his stomach muscles clench.

Her laugh sounded forced. 'You survived without seeing me for eight years, Rafe. How do you suppose we managed that, anyway?' she mused. 'With us both living in Los Angeles and mixing with the same crowd of actor friends and acquaintances?'

Rafe knew exactly how they had avoided meeting each other—whenever he had known Cairo and Lionel were going to be at a party or an awards ceremony, he had avoided going himself, the thought of seeing the two of them together enough to turn his stomach.

'Incredible to believe, isn't it?' he acknowledged dryly.

A miracle, was how Cairo would have described it!

She had lived in nervous trepidation for the first year of her marriage to Lionel just at the thought of accidentally finding herself face to face with Rafe again. But as the months, and then years, had passed without that happening, she had put the idea of it from her mind.

Only for it to happen eight years later at a villa in the South of France, of all places!

'Incredible,' she echoed, before giving Rafe a pointed look.

He nodded. 'It's time I was leaving,' he said. 'But I'm sure it isn't going to be another eight years before the two of us meet again, Cairo,' he promised huskily.

She gave him a startled look. 'You are?'

Rafe shrugged. 'If not before, then we will most certainly see each other again at Simon Raphael's christening.'

Cairo had completely forgotten that Margo and Jeff had earlier asked if the two of them, along with Jeff's brother Neil, would be Simon's godparents.

'Of course,' she acknowledged stiffly. 'I'll—' She broke off the polite adage—she would not look forward to seeing Rafe again, either at the christening or before! 'I'll see you to the door,' she said instead, before crossing the room to open the door for him to leave.

Rafe paused in the open doorway. 'It really has been good to see you again, Cairo.'

'Of course it has,' she came back dryly.

His mouth twisted. 'Cynicism doesn't suit you.'

She shrugged. 'It's a little difficult to be any other way when— Never mind,' she dismissed brightly. 'Have a good flight back to Cannes tomorrow,' she added politely.

Rafe had no intention of going ahead with his original plan of returning to the Cannes Film Festival tomorrow. Not when Pamela Raines, the person he was now determined to talk to, was in Los Angeles….

'Thanks,' Rafe accepted noncommittally.

'You're welcome.'

'Cairo—'

'I'm sure it doesn't usually take you this long to say goodbye, Rafe!' Cairo snapped, her nerves stretched to breaking point. This evening had already been difficult enough without the added strain of this lingering goodbye!

'No,' he acknowledged. 'But, then, this really isn't goodbye, Cairo,' he said, running a single finger down the warmth of her cheek before finally taking his leave.

Cairo hastily closed the door behind him before leaning weakly back against it.

She accepted that there was no way she could get out of being her new nephew's godmother without actually hurting Margo and Jeff's feelings. Nor could she hope that Rafe would change his mind about being godfather to his namesake. But the christening was sure to be weeks, possibly months away—plenty of time for Cairo to have built back her crumbling defences where Rafe was concerned.

She hoped....

CHAPTER TWELVE

'WHO are these roses from?' Cairo asked Josie, the wardrobe lady, as she entered her dressing-room at the theatre on opening night and saw a huge vase of yellow roses in pride of place amongst the other half dozen bouquets that had been delivered.

'There is a card, I believe,' Josie told her distractedly as she examined Cairo's costume for any last-minute problems.

But Cairo didn't need to read the card to know who the yellow roses had come from! Did that mean, despite her having asked him not to, that Rafe was out there in the first-night theatre audience, after all?

Oh, God…!

She sat down abruptly on the chair in front of

the dresser, her hand shaking slightly as she picked the card out from amongst the beautiful yellow blooms and read the words printed on it: 'I believe the correct term is break a leg, but I would really rather you didn't break anything. Will you have supper with me afterwards?'

There was no signature beneath the message, but after their conversation three weeks ago Cairo knew that only Rafe could have sent her the yellow roses.

But why had he?

And why, after Cairo had made it so clear to him that she didn't want to see him alone again, was he inviting her to have supper with him after the play ended?

She wouldn't go, of course.

She couldn't go.

Because, as hard as she had tried, Cairo's response to the arrival of these yellow roses told her that she hadn't managed to rebuild her defences against Rafe in the last three weeks at all!

That perhaps she never would….

* * *

'You were wonderful, Cairo!' Lionel took her in his arms to beam at her proudly once he had managed to make his way to her side through the crowd in her dressing-room.

'Thank you.' Cairo glowed, still too excited by the triumph of the evening to question what her ex-husband was actually doing here.

As she had stood in the wings earlier waiting to make her first entrance a complete calm had come over her, and she had forgotten every-thing—and everyone!—else as she had concen-trated on the performance ahead.

The spontaneous applause, followed by numerous curtain calls, and then the director coming onto the stage to present her with a huge bouquet before hugging and kissing her, had been more than enough to convince her she had succeeded.

'You were right, Cairo, this is where you belong,' Lionel told her ruefully. 'It's a little mad in here right now.' He laughed softly as more people tried to crowd into her dressing-room. 'Will you meet me for lunch tomorrow? I have something important to tell you,' he added persuasively as Cairo started to refuse.

She didn't want to meet with Lionel tomorrow; she had even less to say to him than she did to Rafe, but the genuine appeal in his face was more than she could withstand. 'Okay, Lionel, I'll have lunch with you tomorrow,' she agreed reluctantly.

He grinned his satisfaction. 'One o'clock at Gregory's?' He mentioned the name of the restaurant she'd had dinner at with Rafe three weeks ago.

'One o'clock at Spencer's,' she corrected, opting for a restaurant in which she and Lionel had occasionally dined in the past when they had been in London.

But not so often that it had become 'their' place…

Whatever Lionel had to tell her, she didn't want him to get the wrong idea about her acceptance of this luncheon invitation.

'I really do have to go now, Lionel,' she said, laughing at the loud pop of several champagne bottles being opened.

'Sure you do.' He nodded. 'This is definitely

your night. But I'll look forward to seeing you tomorrow.' He gave her another hug before kissing her lightly on the lips.

Suddenly Cairo became aware of the deadly silence that had fallen over a room that seconds ago had been full of laughter and loud conversation. She stepped back slowly to release herself from Lionel's arms and glanced over towards the door.

Rafe!

He stood in the doorway holding another bottle of champagne, very tall, his dark hair silky, and looking incredibly handsome in a black evening suit, snowy white shirt and black bow tie—and with an expression on that ruggedly arrogant face that was enigmatically unreadable.

The room was full of other members of the cast, the director and backstage crew, as well as family and friends—and all of them, without exception, were staring at the famous actor standing in the doorway of Cairo Vaughn's dressing-room!

'Everybody out, and give Cairo some space,' Paul, the director, called authoritatively even as he began to shoo people out of the room.

'Please don't leave on my account,' Rafe drawled politely.

But it was a politeness that no one, not even Margo and Jeff—the traitors!—took any notice of as Rafe stepped aside and they filed out of Cairo's dressing-room, leaving only Cairo, Lionel, and Rafe—and an awkward silence.

'Time I was going, too,' Lionel remarked, giving Cairo a wry smile before strolling over to the door. He stopped in front of Rafe, the two men looking at each other in silent challenge for several seconds before he spoke again. 'She's too good for both of us, Montero.'

Rafe gave a slight inclination of his head. 'I'm aware of that,' he grated harshly.

'I hope that you are.'

'Lionel—'

'It's okay, Cairo,' Rafe said, before turning back to the older man. 'I'm glad we understand each other,' he said quietly.

Cairo couldn't even begin to understand what had just transpired between the two men, what underlying message their brief conversation had carried—a message that excluded her while somehow being about her.

Men!

'I'll see you at one o'clock tomorrow, Cairo,' Lionel called back, before closing the door behind him as he left.

Cairo was instantly aware of the fact that she was still in the slinky black dress she had worn for the final scene, and that her stage make-up was much too harsh, too overemphasized in the confines of her dressing-room.

'I look a mess.' She turned away to take one of the cleansers from the packet on her dresser before bending down in front of the mirror to begin wiping the make-up from her cheeks. She looked at Rafe's reflection in the mirror. 'Did you see the play? Or have you just arrived?'

'You do not look a mess,' he assured her as he stepped further into the room. 'And, yes, I saw the play. You were magnificent. Wonderful. Electrifying! I doubt a single person took their eyes off you the whole time you were on the stage.'

Pleasure warmed her cheeks. 'I—received the roses, too, thank you.'

He held up the bottle of champagne. 'Do you have any glasses left in here for this or did they take them all away with them?' he asked lightly as he deftly popped the cork on the bottle.

'I have some in here.' She opened the cupboard beneath the dresser. 'What would you have done with this if I'd bombed?' she teased as she held the glasses out for him to pour the champagne into.

'Then I would have collected the second bottle I've got in the car and made sure you became very, very drunk!' Rafe said.

'I think I'm already drunk on success,' she admitted glowingly.

Rafe held up his own glass of champagne. 'To you,' he toasted her huskily. 'You were an absolute triumph tonight, Cairo.' He sipped the champagne, his gaze not leaving the flushed beauty of her face.

He had literally been mesmerized by Cairo the moment she had stepped on the stage earlier tonight, the complete hush that had fallen over the theatre for the whole of her performance, followed by all those curtain calls, telling him that he wasn't alone in his admiration.

He had always known Cairo could act, but tonight, in the setting that she loved best, she had far outshone any of her previous performances on screen.

'I don't want to keep you from the party…' He smiled wryly as he heard the sounds of the rest of the cast and crew still celebrating outside in the hallway.

She laughed. 'It will go on for most of the night, I'm sure.'

'I'm sure of it, too.' Rafe nodded. 'Did I see Margo and Jeff in here a few minutes ago?'

'You did,' Cairo confirmed. 'Rafe, I doubt I'm going to be able to get away for supper for several more hours yet,' she told him apologetically as the noise outside became louder still.

He had already guessed that. But this was Cairo's night and she deserved to enjoy every moment of it.

He smiled reassuringly; at least Cairo hadn't said she didn't want to have supper with him, only that she couldn't right now... 'I thought maybe I would go and have a drink with Margo and Jeff, and the two of us could meet up at my hotel for supper later.'

She grimaced. 'I may not be in any condition to eat supper later!'

'Then I'll just put you to bed and we can have breakfast together in the morning.'

Cairo became very still, sipping her champagne as she thought over what he had just said. Rafe's intention was for them to have supper together at his hotel? Or breakfast! She gave him an overbright smile. 'You could just stay and join in the party?'

'You saw what happened just now...' He shook his head. 'This is your night, Cairo—you don't need Rafe Montero muscling in on the act.'

Her smile widened. 'No doubt it would add to my kudos if he did!'

Rafe threw his head back and laughed. 'Cairo Vaughn doesn't need any added kudos,' he teased.

He seemed different, Cairo realized, frowning at him slightly. Less harsh. With none of that sarcasm and scorn that had been such a part of him when they had met again three weeks ago. But he unnerved her just the same—still making her feel totally aware of him and the response of her own body to his proximity.

Not a good idea!

She deliberately changed the subject. 'Congratulations on winning the Best Director award at Cannes, by the way.' Although, strangely, Cairo had read in the newspapers that Rafe hadn't been there to collect the award himself, after all, that his assistant director had collected it on Rafe's behalf....

'Thank you.' He inclined his head in acknowledgement, the intense blue of his gaze not leaving her face. 'Will you have supper with me later, Cairo? There are some things I need to say to you,' he added gruffly even as Cairo would have made a polite refusal. 'To explain.'

He was hard to resist in this softer, less accusatory mood. More like the Rafe she had known eight years ago. Or the Rafe she had thought she knew, Cairo reminded herself firmly.

She shook her head. 'I really don't think that's a good idea, Rafe.'

He stepped forward to take one of her hands in his and raise it to his lips, his gaze once again holding hers as he pressed a lingering kiss to the back of it. 'Just do this one last thing for me, Cairo,' he begged. 'After that—well, it will be up to you whether or not we see each other again.'

Cairo was totally unnerved now, her hand tingling from the touch of his lips against her skin, every part of her completely aware of him, her breasts feeling full and aroused, the beginnings of warmth between her thighs.

It was the adrenalin, the excitement of a successful opening night, and not Rafe who was the cause of that, she told herself impatiently as she pointedly removed her hand from his. 'Perhaps we could meet some time tomorrow instead?'

He raised an eyebrow. 'I believe you already have a luncheon engagement at one o'clock.'

Cairo had wondered if he had overheard all of her conversation with Lionel. Now she knew.

'We could meet later in the afternoon,' Cairo

offered briskly. 'I don't need to be back at the theatre until seven o'clock in the evening.'

'If that's the best you can do.'

He couldn't exactly blame Cairo for her reluctance to meet and talk with him again. Not after the way he had treated her three weeks ago!

She looked at him searchingly. 'Rafe, what's all this about?'

Rafe debated how much to tell her now. This was hardly the time or the place for the conversation he wanted to have with Cairo, and he should have realized that before writing the message on the card he'd had delivered with the yellow roses.

He straightened. 'Redemption, Cairo,' he admitted huskily. 'It's about redemption.'

Her eyes widened, her expression wary. 'Now you really have intrigued me, Rafe,' she said slowly.

'Enough to change your mind about supper?'

She hesitated. 'Maybe,' she finally allowed cautiously.

Rafe smiled. 'I have a suite at The Ritz if you should decide to join me later, after all…'

She would be stupid to do so, Cairo knew. Stupid, as well as certifiably insane. But then, her feelings for Rafe had never been exactly sane in the first place!

'We'll see,' she answered noncommittally. 'Although it could be very late,' she added as the revelry outside seemed to become even louder.

'Any time will be fine.'

Cairo really was intrigued by this conversation, couldn't even begin to imagine what Rafe wanted to talk to her about. But the question was, was she intrigued enough to put herself in the position of joining Rafe at his hotel later on tonight—or tomorrow morning?

Her brain told her a firm no.

But her heart—and every other tinglingly aware part of her—said yes!

'As I said, we'll see,' she repeated. 'Now, if you wouldn't mind, I have to change before joining the others….'

It was the best he could hope for, Rafe knew. In fact, in the circumstances, it was more than he had hoped for!

He knew now that he bore a large part of the blame for Cairo having been hurt enough eight years ago to end their relationship. Pamela might have been the instrument of that hurt, but Cairo had only been twenty; he'd been sophisticated enough in the ways of women, had known Pamela well enough, to have foreseen what had happened and stopped it before Cairo had become involved, too. Then getting drunk and sleeping with Pamela on Cairo's wedding day had only confused matters even more—he should never have done that as it had given Pamela even more ammunition against Cairo.

'Of course,' he accepted lightly. 'Enjoy the rest of your party, Cairo—you deserve it.'

But Cairo didn't enjoy the party, or the club they all spilled out to once they had left the theatre; instead she remained totally distracted by her earlier conversation with Rafe and could think of little else.

Why did Rafe need redemption?

Or perhaps it wasn't his own redemption he had been referring to…?

CHAPTER THIRTEEN

IT WAS almost three o'clock in the morning when Rafe opened the door of his hotel suite to Cairo, although the challenging expression on her face as she swept past him and into the sitting-room wasn't exactly encouraging.

She looked gorgeous, of course, her hair loose down the length of her spine, the green off-the-shoulder, knee-length dress clinging to all of her beautiful curves, the sheerness of the material clearly outlining the firm thrust of her breasts. Her legs were long and silky smooth, her feet thrust into matching green high-heeled sandals.

Gorgeous and very self assured—and not a little annoyed, Rafe acknowledged ruefully as he saw the flush of anger in her cheeks and her glittering eyes as she stood facing him across the room.

'Would you like to sit down?' he invited.

'I'm not staying,' she snapped.

She was very annoyed, Rafe realized regretfully. Mainly with him, but a little with herself, he would guess—for having come here at all....

'Have you had enough champagne or would you care for some more?' He indicated the bottle he'd had cooling in an ice-bucket on the table for the last two hours, along with two fluted glasses.

Cairo eyed Rafe impatiently, most of that impatience directed at herself as she felt herself responding to how devastatingly handsome he looked.

His overlong dark hair was slightly tousled, as if he had been running his fingers through it before she arrived, and he had removed his dinner jacket and bow tie, the white silk evening shirt fitting perfectly over his wide shoulders, the black trousers tailored to powerful hips and the long length of his legs.

'No, thanks,' she refused. 'As I said, I'm not staying.' She looked at him narrowly. 'You made an intriguing remark earlier, Rafe—something about redemption?—and I want to know what you meant by it.'

He grimaced. 'Do you mind if I have some?' He indicated the champagne.

'Knock yourself out.'

This was going to be harder than he had imagined, Rafe thought as he moved to uncork the bottle and poured some of the pink champagne into a glass, taking a slow sip before turning back to face her.

At twenty Cairo had been very young, as well as very naïve and trusting; now she was eight years older and looked as if she trusted very little any more—especially anything to do with him!

'It's very late, Rafe,' she pointed out as she moved to do what she had said she didn't want to do, and sat down in one of the armchairs. 'And I really am very tired.' She gave a weary sigh, leant her head back against the chair and closed her eyes.

Rafe could see the truth of that now that her cheeks were no longer flushed and he couldn't see her eyes sparkling with temper. Also, that air of vulnerability he had noticed about her three weeks ago was back in evidence.

An impression that was instantly dispelled as she opened her eyes and straightened in the chair, ready for the attack. 'So, what did you want to say to me, Rafe?'

So much. And yet so little. The whole sum of what Rafe wanted to say to Cairo could be said in three words. Just three little words. But he was getting ahead of himself, he cautioned; Cairo would probably laugh in his face if he said those particular words to her now without bothering to explain....

He moved to sit in the chair opposite hers. 'First of all we have to go back eight years—'

'Why do we?' She tensed. 'It was all so long ago, and surely has no bearing on our lives now?'

'It has every bearing on here and now,' he insisted. 'Cairo, when I left you three weeks ago, instead of returning to Cannes, I flew back to the States.'

So that was why he hadn't been in Cannes to collect his award himself, Cairo realized guardedly. But what of it? What possible interest could it be to her what Rafe had done three weeks ago, or at any other time, for that matter?

Rafe's mouth was a thin, uncompromising line. 'Cairo, I went back to Los Angeles to see Pamela Raines—'

'Rafe, I don't want to know who you went to see!' Cairo told him forcefully as she stood up in an immediate reaction to hearing that name. 'You are unbelievable, do you know that?' She glared at him. 'Not content with having interrupted my holiday with Daisy, you've now ruined my first night back at the theatre, too, with your enigmatic requests to talk to me! Why don't you go and ruin someone else's life, Rafe, and just stay out of mine?' She was breathing hard with the strength of her emotions. 'Damn you,' she finally bit out furiously. 'How *dare* you come here and talk to me about Pamela Raines?'

He sat forward in his chair, his expression grim. 'Cairo, I'm trying to tell you that I did not, nor did I ever, have an affair with Pamela Raines.

I only ever slept with her that one time on your wedding day—'

'That's a lie, Rafe,' she interrupted angrily.

'No. No, it isn't.'

'You were having an affair with her while you were still seeing me, dammit!'

'I know now that *you* thought I was—'

'I didn't *think* anything, Rafe. Nor did I imagine it,' Cairo assured him icily. 'I finished filming early one morning and came to your hotel suite. She— Pamela answered the door. She was stark naked— The bed was a mess— Her clothes were all over the floor—'

'But where were *my* clothes, Cairo?' he put in softly.

'I—well—wherever you were, you were obviously wearing them!' she dismissed with a wave of her hand. 'What does it matter where your clothes were, Rafe?' She scowled at him darkly. 'What matters is that you were obviously *not* wearing them a short time before I arrived so unexpectedly, because you and Pamela had been— God, it still makes me feel ill to know that you—

that you were sleeping with both of us at the same time!'

Rafe gave a parody of a smile. 'Now probably isn't the right time to point out that what you thought I was doing with both of you had nothing to do with *sleeping*….'

Cairo's eyes narrowed to livid slits. 'Not unless you want me to hit you over the head with that champagne bottle, no!'

Rafe's smile became a little more genuine. 'Perhaps you should have done that after you thought you had caught me out with Pamela? At least that way we could have talked this through when I woke up!'

'I could no more have sat down and talked with you about your affair with Pamela then than I can now—'

'There was *no* affair, Cairo,' Rafe repeated firmly. 'Not then. And most certainly not now.'

'You—'

'Not now. And certainly *not* eight years ago,' Rafe reiterated evenly, his gaze steadily holding hers. 'Pamela had made it more than obvious that was what she wanted, but I wasn't interested.'

His mouth twisted self-derisively. 'I was only interested in the red-haired witch who had knocked me off my feet the very first moment I looked at her…You, Cairo,' he added so that there should be absolutely no doubt in her mind.

Cairo looked at him searchingly for several long seconds, seeing only sincerity in his expression. Sincerity and a plea for her to believe him.

'So you didn't go to bed with her that morning?'

'I didn't,' Rafe said patiently. 'In fact, until you mentioned it three weeks ago, I'd had no idea that that was what you had always believed.'

'But I know what I saw, Rafe,' Cairo pointed out. 'So how do you explain it?'

He stood up restlessly. 'It was only when you insisted that I had been involved with Pamela for weeks that I even suspected— Don't you understand, Cairo? What you saw in my hotel room was totally engineered by Pamela!'

Cairo shook her head in denial. 'Don't think you can make a fool of me again, Rafe—'

'I assure you I'm not trying to do that.' Rafe sighed. 'That morning at the hotel Pamela charmed one of the housemaids into letting her into my suite before throwing off all her clothes and just sitting there waiting for me to return, absolutely sure that once I did, I wouldn't be able to resist her.' He grimaced. 'Unfortunately, you came to my hotel suite before I did. But, never one to lose an opportunity, Pamela rethought her plan and deliberately turned the situation to her advantage by giving you the impression that she and I had spent the morning in bed together and that I'd been cheating on you with her for weeks!'

Cairo stared at him, sure that what Rafe was saying was too fantastic to be true. And yet, at the same time, it was too fantastic to have been made up, either!

She swallowed hard. 'Why would she do something like that?'

'Pamela is well known for wanting—and getting—her own way. For having any man she wants. When she made it obvious that she wanted me, I tried to let her know I wasn't interested. But

I should have known—should have guessed—that Pamela wouldn't just accept that, that she would do something. I had absolutely no idea what had happened that morning at the hotel, Cairo, which is why I was so totally stunned when we met for lunch and you told me it was over between us. If I'd been thinking more clearly, I should have realised immediately that something was wrong—that you must have had a reason for doing what you did.'

It was incredible!

So incredible it just might be true…?

But if Rafe hadn't been involved in an affair with Pamela Raines eight years ago, after all…

Cairo looked across at the man she had once loved. At the man she still loved! She moistened her lips with the tip of her tongue. 'Is all of that really true, Rafe?'

'I swear that it is,' he breathed raggedly. 'The only time I ever stupidly slept with her was because I had already drunk myself practically into insensibility on your wedding day.'

'What a mess,' she groaned.

'Yes,' Rafe agreed. 'We've wasted *eight years*, Cairo. Eight long years!'

They had been just as long for Cairo, most of them spent married to a man she could no longer trust, let alone love.

'Where do we go from here?' Rafe asked as she continued to stay silent. Why didn't she say something?

Anything!

Because her silence, now that she knew the truth, was killing him….

She gave him a sad smile. 'I don't see that we go anywhere, Rafe.'

He frowned darkly. 'Why don't you?'

She shrugged. 'Obviously Pamela Raines's lies precipitated the end of our relationship, but I very much doubt that it would have lasted much longer anyway—'

'How can you say that, Cairo?' Rafe rasped fiercely, his hands clenching at his sides. 'How can you possibly *know* that?'

'Well, I don't, of course,' she allowed. 'But I think it's safe to say that our lives were as different then as they are now. You're the famous Rafe Montero—'

'You're the equally famous Cairo Vaughn!'

Cairo grimaced. 'It's taken me years to become her, Rafe. When we first met, I was only just starting out, was a relative unknown. It's only been through hard work that I've made a name for myself.'

Rafe looked at her searchingly. 'Why did you work so hard, Cairo? Why have you made one movie after another, back-to-back sometimes, never seeming to take a break, and always on show, your photograph constantly in one magazine or another?'

Her expression became guarded. 'You seem to forget that I've taken a break the last ten months,' she reminded him stiffly. 'Besides, didn't *you* tell me three weeks ago that I needed to get back to work in order that the public didn't forget me?'

Yes, he had told her that. But the coincidence of her taking a break from her career following her parting from Lionel Bond was too obvious to pass without comment....

'Was your marriage to Bond all you hoped it would be, Cairo?' Rafe pursued.

'Obviously not, as we've recently divorced,' she commented unhelpfully.

'But you were married to him for over seven years—'

'Rafe, I'm—happy, to have learnt what really happened eight years ago, but that doesn't entitle you to know anything about my marriage to Lionel,' Cairo said defensively as she bent to pick up her evening bag from where she had earlier placed it on the arm of the chair. 'In fact, I think it's probably time I left—'

'Cairo, that morning I had gone out shopping to buy you an engagement ring!'

Cairo froze.

Absolutely froze.

Rafe couldn't really have just said—he *couldn't* have—

'It's here, Cairo,' he continued raggedly as he picked up his discarded evening jacket to take a small ring-box from one of the pockets. 'There's even the receipt here to show you the date that I bought it.' He held up a neatly folded piece of paper.

Cairo straightened abruptly to eye him in complete shock. Rafe had bought her an *engagement ring* eight years ago?

'That day—' He broke off, briefly closing his eyes before opening them again to look at her. 'I had intended asking you to marry me when we went out to lunch that day, and I had the ring in my pocket to give you if you said yes. But before I could do so, you told me it was all over between us!' He shook his head. 'I was too stunned—was hurting too badly—to even question why you were doing it. By the time I had recovered my senses enough to need those answers, you were already going out with Bond. Then when you announced your engagement to him so quickly, it made, as I thought, any explanations between the two of us completely unnecessary.'

Cairo stared at him, unmoving, almost not breathing.

Rafe's mouth twisted. 'Don't worry, I haven't carried the ring around with me for years like some lovesick puppy—in fact, if we had still been in the Isle of Man at the time I would probably have hurled the damn thing into the Irish Sea! But I did keep it, Cairo,' he added huskily. 'If only as a reminder to myself of just how fickle love can be.'

Cairo swallowed, the blood pounding through her veins so loudly it almost deafened her. '*Love*, Rafe…?' she finally managed to ask faintly.

His expression softened. 'I was completely, deeply in love with you, Cairo. I knew that I wanted to spend the rest of my life with you.'

And instead only weeks later Cairo had married another man!

Because she had believed Pamela Raines's lies.

Because Cairo had been so young and unsure of herself that she had believed the other woman when she'd taunted her that she could never hope to hold the interest of a man like Rafe Montero.

She moistened her lips with the tip of her tongue. 'That—that's simply unbelievable, Rafe.'

'It's the truth, dammit!' Rafe barked forcefully, his eyes gleaming fiercely. 'Look at the ring if you don't believe me, Cairo.' He snapped the box open and thrust it towards her, revealing a huge emerald surrounded by six only slightly smaller diamonds. 'You once told me that emeralds were your favourite stone,' he added gruffly.

Yes, she had. But she had never thought—never believed—Rafe had been in love with her eight years ago! Or that he had been going to ask her to marry him!

'It's beautiful,' she whispered emotionally.

'I thought so,' he agreed, before closing the lid of the box and throwing it down on the table. 'At least now perhaps you can understand some of my more—bitter accusations, concerning your sudden marriage to Bond.'

Cairo understood only too well.

But what did she do next?

These explanations about the past were all very well, but they gave her no clues as to how Rafe felt about her now!

'To answer your earlier question, Rafe—no, my marriage to Lionel wasn't anything like I had hoped it would be,' she told him woodenly.

Rafe eyed her guardedly, not wanting to read more into her statement than was intended. The problem was, he had no idea what Cairo intended! But she had deserved to know the truth about eight years ago. All of it, including the fact that Rafe had been in love with her and wanted to marry her.

Cairo shook her head. 'How could it possibly be a happy marriage when I had married him while still in love with another man?'

Rafe felt his heart lift. 'Cairo—'

'No, let me finish, Rafe,' she told him with quiet firmness. 'I told you three weeks ago that I couldn't tell you any of this without breaking a confidence, but I believe, after what you've just told me, that I at least owe you some explanation in return. I married Lionel because he asked me to, and because I was still absolutely devastated by what I had thought was your betrayal. It wasn't a bad marriage. Lionel and I got on well enough to start with, neither of us making demands that the other couldn't give.' She shrugged. 'I'm sure that lots of marriages have survived with less,' she added ruefully.

Rafe wasn't sure he wanted to hear all of this now that Cairo actually wanted to tell him. Just the thought of her being with Lionel Bond, of her marriage to him, had tied Rafe up in knots for months, years, afterwards, to the point that he had never been able to fully trust or love another woman.

Cairo continued, 'We would probably have continued to survive if I hadn't learned of Lionel's gambling habit. More like an obsession, really,' she corrected heavily. 'I'd had no idea when I married him, but only months later I discovered that he gambled every dollar he could spare. A couple of years into our marriage he was so hooked that he began to gamble dollars he didn't even have.' She sighed. 'It didn't really matter, of course, because I had started to earn big money by that time, and by working almost exclusively for Lionel's production company I also put more money back into his bank account, too.'

'*That's* the reason you've been working so hard all these years?' Rafe realised furiously.

She nodded. 'I blamed myself, you see,

because although I liked Lionel I—I simply couldn't love him.' She avoided Rafe's searching gaze, determined to finish this now that she had started. 'When Lionel realized how deeply he had become addicted, we were still friends enough for him to feel he could come to me and confess all.' She shook her head. 'He promised me that he would stop.'

'But he didn't,' Rafe said slowly.

'No.' She sighed. 'He just became more secretive about it. Maybe I should have realized sooner, I don't know. But it's very hard to maintain a balanced relationship in a marriage when you have to constantly watch your partner in case he lapses back into a destructive habit. As it turned out, I didn't watch Lionel nearly close enough. Part of my trusting him was having a joint bank account with him, and—about a year ago—I discovered that he had been secretly taking money out of that account, too, and using that to gamble—and lose—with.'

'Leaving you broke, too?' Rafe asked shrewdly.

She gave a sad smile. 'Not quite. I wasn't

stupid enough to put all that I earned in our joint account, and I have worked very hard over the last few years, Rafe. I really tried to save our marriage, too, but after the incident with the joint bank account I realized that nothing I did or said was going to make Lionel stop. There was also the hope that by putting an end to our marriage I might shock him into stopping,' she admitted.

'And did it?'

'It would appear not,' Cairo said flatly. 'When he came to the villa that day it was to ask me for money—'

'That's what you meant when you said it wasn't actually you that Bond wanted back?' Rafe interrupted.

'Yes.'

'You didn't give him any more money, did you?' he burst out angrily.

All these years—all this time, he had thought Cairo was at least happy with the choice she had made! Now it seemed she had no more been happy than he had!

'No, I didn't,' she confirmed heavily. 'It was

hard to say no to him, because—because I've always felt that it was because I didn't love him, couldn't love him, that his obsession with gambling intensified after our marriage—'

'That's ridiculous, Cairo,' Rafe cut in harshly.

'Is it?' She frowned. 'I became a workaholic in order to paper over the cracks in my marriage, so why shouldn't it have increased Lionel's obsession with gambling?'

'Because we're all ultimately responsible for our own actions,' Rafe reasoned. 'Hell, I lost the woman I loved, and that made me extremely unhappy, and very wary of ever falling in love again, but it certainly didn't turn me into a workaholic or an obsessive gambler!'

'No.' She smiled wryly. 'But you're a much stronger man than Lionel.'

'You think?' Rafe bit out.

'I *know* you are, Rafe,' she said softly.

'What else do you know about me, Cairo?' he said emotionally. 'For instance, do you know that I still love you? That in all these years I've never stopped loving you? Not even for a moment?'

'You still love me…?' Cairo stared at him in shock as the full force of what Rafe had just said hit her like a physical blow.

Rafe nodded. 'I always have. From the very first moment I saw you.'

'But you never said—you didn't tell me!'

'I was a fool,' he rasped. 'You were perfect, unbelievable, and for three months it all seemed too good to be true. We had an incredible physical chemistry between us, but I thought it was too much to hope that you might feel more for me than that, that perhaps you might come to love me in return. But then I decided to hell with it, I would tell you anyway, and then ask you to marry me; the worst thing that could happen was that you would turn me down.'

'I would have said yes!'

He closed his eyes briefly. 'Don't tell me that, Cairo, it only makes it worse!'

'But I loved you, too, Rafe,' she admitted huskily. 'I loved you so much!'

'Loved, Cairo?' he said painfully. 'Past tense?'

Her own tears were blinding her, and her legs

felt decidedly shaky. Trying to swallow past a huge lump in her throat, for a moment Cairo couldn't speak.

'Cairo, will you please at least answer me?' Rafe ordered.

She drew in a trembling breath, knowing by the almost defensive expression on Rafe's face that he actually feared what that answer might be. 'I still love you, too, Rafe,' she admitted, her gaze steady on his. 'I've never stopped loving you. Not for a single moment of the last eight years!' she choked even as she threw herself into his arms, her hands cupping each side of his face as she kissed him over and over again. 'I love you, Rafe!' She smiled shakily, her eyes glowing with the emotion. 'I love you! I love you!'

Those same three little words that Rafe knew he should have said to her long ago but hadn't! The same three words that would now bind them together for a lifetime. Because he never intended letting anything, or anyone, come between the two of them ever again!

'I still love you, too, Cairo,' he groaned as his

arms clamped about her like steel bands and he held her tightly against him. 'I've never stopped loving you, either.'

'Never, Rafe?'

'Never,' he repeated fiercely. 'I used to see photographs of you in magazines, newspapers, usually with Bond, and each time I did it was like a twist in my gut, an agony I couldn't bear.'

Cairo shook her head. 'That was the life Lionel wanted us to lead, not me. I put up with it, felt it was the least I could do when I had so little else to give him, but really I hated all that artificiality. Parties. Premieres.' She gave a shudder. 'I didn't enjoy it at all. The only consolation was that I never had to actually meet you at any of them,' she admitted.

'Deliberately so,' Rafe told her huskily. 'I stayed away on purpose, Cairo,' he explained as she looked up at him with an obvious query in her eyes. 'I just couldn't stand the thought of seeing you and Bond together,' he acknowledged heavily.

Cairo's gaze became searching as she saw the

truth of his words in his face. 'Oh, Rafe, what fools we've been!' she groaned achingly.

'But no more,' he vowed. 'I love you, Cairo, and I know without a doubt that I always will,' he promised. 'Will you marry me?'

'Oh, yes,' she breathed raggedly. 'Yes, yes, *yes*!'

Rafe gave a shout of triumphant laughter as he gathered her even closer in his arms, and then his mouth claimed hers.

Cairo, the woman he had loved, did love, would always love…

'We're getting married as soon as we can get a licence,' Rafe told her determinedly a long time later. They were lying in bed together, Rafe's arms wrapped tightly around Cairo as her head rested on his bare shoulder, her fingers played teasingly with the dark hair on his chest, both of them flushed and satiated from making beautiful love together.

Cairo smiled dreamily. 'You won't hear any arguments against that idea from me,' she murmured.

Mrs Rafe Montero.

Mrs Raphael Antonio Miguel Montero.

It sounded wonderful!

It would *be* wonderful.

She and Rafe had been through too much, had loved each other for so long in spite of everything, and Cairo had no doubts that they would continue to love each other for the rest of their lives. Which reminded her…

She raised her head to look down at him with clear brown eyes. 'I love you very much, Rafe.'

'Never, ever doubt that I love you,' he responded forcefully, blue eyes glittering with the emotion. 'Never, Cairo!'

She never would, for she knew now that the love she and Rafe felt for each other was a love for all time….

EPILOGUE

'NOT giving you ideas, is it, Mrs Montero?' Rafe teased huskily as Cairo handed four-month-old baby Simon back to Margo as they all left the church following the christening.

'And if it is?' Cairo gave him one of those enigmatic smiles that always made Rafe want to take her to bed.

As did her laugh. And her rare—nowadays—frown. And her thoughtful look. Hell, Rafe just enjoyed taking Cairo to bed, no matter what her expression!

The two of them had made their lifetime vows two and a half months ago, with only Rafe's parents, his brother and his family, and Margo, Jeff and the children in attendance.

It had been ten lovely weeks of being together

constantly whenever Cairo wasn't at the theatre. Now Cairo's very successful run was over, the two of them intended to return next week to Rafe's house at the beach.

Rafe slid his arm possessively about Cairo's waist. 'I can't imagine anything I would enjoy more than to see you growing big with our child,' he admitted throatily.

Cairo leant into him to murmur, 'Then stop imagining it, Rafe.'

His eyes widened as he looked down at her. 'You mean— Cairo, are you—?'

She chuckled softly at his dumbstruck expression. 'I do. And I am. Seven weeks, according to Margo's doctor.'

Cairo had never felt so happy in her life as she had been this last three months with Rafe, ten weeks of it as his wife, and the knowledge that she now carried their child was almost overwhelming.

Even the shadow of Lionel had been removed from her life, the 'important' thing he had wanted to tell her over lunch that day turning out to be his decision to book himself into a clinic, a condition of his engagement to the movie director Sarah Wallis. Cairo knew Sarah slightly, had worked with her in the past, and knew her to be tough and single-minded; if Sarah had decided that Lionel wouldn't gamble any more, then Cairo had no doubts that he wouldn't.

As the two of them were to be married next month, it seemed that Sarah had got her way!

Cairo shot Rafe a teasing look now. 'Of course, it means I may have to take a few months off work once we've finished filming *Forgiveness* together…' For the first time in years, the two of them were to work together again, Cairo in the lead role, Rafe as director, something they were both looking forward to immensely.

'Cairo, I don't give a damn whether you ever work again,' he told her happily.

'But the public might forget me,' she teased him.

'You belong to me—and our baby—not the public,' he stated arrogantly.

Cairo chuckled. 'I love you very much, Rafe Montero.'

'And I love you, Mrs Rafe Montero,' he

murmured huskily as he turned to take her in his arms. 'Till my dying breath,' he promised gruffly as his mouth claimed hers and the two of them forgot everyone, and everything, but each other….

MILLS & BOON PUBLISH EIGHT LARGE PRINT TITLES A MONTH. THESE ARE THE EIGHT TITLES FOR JULY 2009.

CAPTIVE AT THE SICILIAN BILLIONAIRE'S COMMAND
Penny Jordan

THE GREEK'S MILLION-DOLLAR BABY BARGAIN
Julia James

BEDDED FOR THE SPANIARD'S PLEASURE
Carole Mortimer

AT THE ARGENTINEAN BILLIONAIRE'S BIDDING
India Grey

ITALIAN GROOM, PRINCESS BRIDE
Rebecca Winters

FALLING FOR HER CONVENIENT HUSBAND
Jessica Steele

CINDERELLA'S WEDDING WISH
Jessica Hart

THE REBEL HEIR'S BRIDE
Patricia Thayer

MILLS & BOON®
Pure reading pleasure™

MILLS & BOON PUBLISH EIGHT LARGE PRINT TITLES A MONTH. THESE ARE THE EIGHT TITLES FOR AUGUST 2009.

———————————— ભ ————————————

THE SPANISH BILLIONAIRE'S PREGNANT WIFE
Lynne Graham

THE ITALIAN'S RUTHLESS MARRIAGE COMMAND
Helen Bianchin

THE BRUNELLI BABY BARGAIN
Kim Lawrence

THE FRENCH TYCOON'S PREGNANT MISTRESS
Abby Green

DIAMOND IN THE ROUGH
Diana Palmer

SECRET BABY, SURPRISE PARENTS
Liz Fielding

THE REBEL KING
Melissa James

NINE-TO-FIVE BRIDE
Jennie Adams